Nightshade

The Nightshade Saga: Book One

Evelyn Lederman

Dedicated to my mother, Carla Singer Lederman. She was born in Germany in 1925, as a German Jew. Barely escaping with their lives, Carla came to this country in 1939 with her own mother. Before coming to the United States, she witnessed first-hand that monsters can live outside the Nightshade Universe. She did not live to see one of my books published, but I knew she would have gotten a kick out of them.

Prologue

The Nightshade Universe

He was older than dirt, Drake thought after the lovely blonde who stood before him asked his age. How do you explain the unexplainable? Drake's existence defied nature.

This was one of the rare occasions he wished he was something other than what he was. His kind was a blight on any world they inhabited. A mistake, never intended to exist in this or any other universe.

At the beginning of time, as worlds fractured across dimensions, a division went terribly wrong. A sentient energy was forged rather than coming to life organically. The oddity traveled between worlds, leaving holes of negative matter in its wake. These frequency pathways between universes were never intended to exist.

As the energy mass traveled, it drew on the life-force of living particles. When it came across man, it claimed its first victim as a shell to occupy.

After settling into the primitive brain and physiology, it evolved from draining a being's life-force to drinking the fluid carrying the elements needed to regenerate the fragile biological cells, allowing the body to physically continue.

Thus, the first vampire came to be.

Drake had been one of the first men the vampire converted. For eons Drake traveled with this creature, living off the blood of others. Over time they converted worthy victims to join their family. Since women had the ability to reproduce, they only changed the male of the species. As a sense of ennui set in, more of the sacrificed were changed into vampires. The newly made helped to relieve the boredom of immortality.

The vampires grew weary of being intergalactic nomads. Eventually they settled in the Nightshade universe. Satisfied within their own world, the knowledge to manipulate matter to travel between universes was lost. Thus, only the original retained the ability.

There had been so many world divisions since his making, Drake had no idea which world had been his birthplace. It was best not to think along those lines. The ones he left behind had long been in their graves. Their progeny would no longer have known he ever existed. His life was now tied to his creator. The entity seemed content to stay in the Nightshade universe, while Drake had nowhere else to go.

The numerous portals leading to the Nightshade universe provided enough unfortunate beings pulled into their world to offer ample sustenance. Blood was plentiful in those early days. The maker was comfortable living off the unlimited supply of blood, until a woman came through one of the portals and life as they knew it changed.

She had a type of power over his creator Drake had never witnessed before. Her presence seemed to relieve the constant hunger the entity suffered. The master referred to her as his soul mate.

Through their bonding, the master thought he would transform into whatever nature had originally planned. They would venture off together, sometimes disappearing for weeks. Finally, one day the master left through a portal with the woman, never to be seen or heard from again.

After his departure, various legends related to their destined pairing began to be told. Over time, most vampires chose to ignore and ultimately forgot those stories. However, in Drake's darkest times, the thought of one day finding his own soul mate made him persevere.

Over several millennia the numerous portals started to close, until only three were active in the Nightshade universe. The vampire population had become so large, and the blood sources so scarce, most were shadows of what they once were.

Now blood frenzied creatures, they slowly wasted away. No amount of blood could regenerate those beings back into what they once were. Only the vampires who had been created by the master, had been spared the horrible thirst. Their bodies were as they were when they were first transformed. Drake held on to what little humanity he had left, waiting for his soul mate to become reality. Through her, Drake could finally transform from the parasite he was.

The woman in front of him was someone else's soul mate. She had the ability to navigate portals using her telepathic abilities and a crystal. The woman, Shirl, had entered their world and was now being held captive. Drake took the opportunity to offer his protection, capitalizing on the opportunity to spend time with the beauty. He had abused his role as a guest within the Venture Hive, to possess the woman for whatever time he could have with her.

Drake manipulated the telepathic bond that tied Shirl to her soul mate. Until he was forced to give her up, he would hold on to her with every fiber of his being. She was as close as he had ever come to finding his own soul mate.

What little happiness he currently had would be cut short when the daughter of the Venture Hive's master was exchanged for Shirl. Everything would be lost if Afton returned to the Nightshade universe.

Chapter 1

⁓

Ginkgo Terra/Earth

It was all a matter of perspective. The abundance of fall color surrounding her could be taken as natural beauty or a sign of death. Darkness had surrounded Afton Simmons most of her life. She chose the positive view when one of her black moods was not upon her. Today was so beautiful, she figured no one could be depressed. Her eyes basked on yellow, orange, and red leaves still attached to the grove of maple trees before her.

Afton loved the mythical story of Persephone to explain the changing of the seasons. When Persephone returned to Hades in the Underworld, her mother Demeter would mourn her daughter's loss by causing all living plants to go dormant, until her daughter returned to her. It was a lovely story of motherly devotion, something foreign to Afton.

Her mother had taken her own life when Afton was barely three years old. An irreversible reaction to the death of the man she loved and an inability to recover from the circumstances of Afton's conception. No wonder Afton spent most of her existence in a sorrowful mood.

Nana, her grandmother, had spent a fortune taking her to one psychiatrist after another. Years of therapy hardly made a dent in on-going depressions. Even the medications they had given her made no difference. In addition, the side effects the anti-depressants caused were worse than her dark moods.

Her last class was over and she had the weekend to look forward to. Her art class was going to Morton's Arboretum tomorrow to capture the autumn colors on canvas. She was also taking the day off from studying. The freedom of spending a day without keeping her nose to the grindstone put an extra spring into her step. Her first semester at Northwestern University was turning out to be tougher than she had originally thought.

When she reached her dorm, she took two steps at a time as she ran up the back stairs. Afton felt absolutely wonderful. She was going to do her economics homework and then treat herself to an episode of *Sherlock*. Benedict Cumberbatch pushed all the right buttons as far as she was concerned. He was tall, handsome, and she loved his wavy hair. For some reason she thought the long, curly locks made him look vulnerable.

Why couldn't she find someone like him? Men tended to shy away from her pale, delicate looks. The boys had been cruel over the years describing her fragile state. Afton shook her head, driving out the names she had been called. She would not let the past drag her into a dour mood.

Once she reached her dorm room, she unlocked the door. Afton was fortunate to get a single room. Her "medical condition" allowed her the luxury of housing alone, such a privilege was normally not available to freshmen.

She made her way to the fridge. It had been modified with a locking mechanism. If anyone asked about the refrigerator, she told them she was diabetic. Her supposed dependency on insulin made locking it a necessity. Afton even had syringes to add credence to her story.

She unlocked the padlock and opened her fridge to reveal its true contents. Blood.

She had been dependent on her liquid diet for as long as she could remember. With all the food allergies people suffered, no one thought twice about her not taking meals in the dorm's cafeteria. Solid food was indigestible by her system. It had been years since she had tried to consume solid food due to her system's violent reaction each time she attempted to eat.

Fortunately, she was able to drink just about anything. It made her feel less of an oddity around her peers. She was able to have a soda or beer with a classmate, allowing her somewhat of a social life. Unfortunately, the caloric content did nothing to add flesh to her bones or give her energy. Only blood would satisfy the needs of her body.

Nana had told Afton she had taken her to see doctors when she was a baby to determine what was wrong with her, but that had been a lie. When she was older, Afton was told the truth about her heritage and why she required blood.

Afton always concentrated on fulfilling her body's need for the crimson liquid, and not on *why* she needed this specific nutrient. The reason was closer to a horror novel than the true story of her mother falling through some type of portal in Sedona, Arizona into a realm of vampires who existed in a parallel universe.

That world filled her re-occurring nightmares. Having been a baby when her mother and she had been rescued, Afton had no idea if what she saw in her nightmares were true memories or a construct of what she imagined such a place would look like.

She'd just settled in to study when a knock on her door caused her to jump in her chair. She got up to see who had come to visit. It was usually the Resident Assistant sharing some information about a policy change. To her surprise, a girl about her age was standing in front of her. She had a healthy tan, where Afton was as pale as death.

"Hi," the vision of health greeted her. "My name is Cassie Clark. I am coming here next semester and visiting the campus. Would you mind showing me your room? I managed to snag a single like yours. My dad knows some Northwestern University hotshot." The girl talked so fast, Afton was not sure she even breathed between words.

"Sure," she stepped aside to allow the girl to enter. Her black hair seemed dull compared to Cassie's vibrant mahogany colored tresses. It shone even in the artificial light. Afton had to stop comparing herself to this beautiful girl, it would sour her good mood.

Cassie walked around her small dorm room and glanced at her when she came upon the locked refrigerator. "I am diabetic," Afton answered the questioning look.

"My best friend at home is diabetic," Cassie replied. Although Afton did not have the disease, she felt less of an oddball. "Would you like to grab a diet soda or something? My dad, older brother, and some of his friends are scouting the campus with me. They are all really cute!" The girl had such an inviting smile on her face.

Afton usually turned down such invitations, but for some reason she really wanted to go. Meeting some nice looking, sweet guy would be nice. Pressure was building in her head, which was weird because she had never been sick a day in her life. What a terrible time to have her first headache.

The temperature in the room must have been set higher than usual, since she felt a trickle of perspiration running down her lip. Brushing it with her hand, she was surprised to see blood on her index finger. Afton looked at Cassie to see if she had noticed her nose bleed.

It must have been her imagination, but for a second, Cassie had a guilty look on her face. When she registered the expression in her mind and checked again, only a look of concern was on the girl's face.

"Let me grab you some tissues," Cassie said, reaching for a nearby box. "The air has been so dry, my brother had a similar episode this morning." It sounded like a logical explanation, certainly better than the thoughts of doom that flew through her head.

"I would love to go," Afton told Cassie. Instantaneously her headache disappeared. It must have been her sub-conscious pushing her to be more social. Besides, she needed to buy a six-pack of spring water, since she downed the last bottle before she headed to her last class. Over time she realized she needed less blood if she was properly hydrated.

As they walked to meet Cassie's party, they talked about insignificant things. Afton really hoped that Cassie would be coming to Northwestern next semester. She did not have any friends and had instantly liked this girl. Maybe she would make a connection with Cassie's brother or one of his friends. She did not realize how truly lonely she was until she started to interact with her possible new friend.

"They are across the street under the streetlamp. Dad," Cassie yelled across the street to grab her father's attention. A good looking man in his early forties with graying sable hair turned around. Next to him was a tall, lanky man with sun-bleached hair. Afton figured the Adonis was Cassie's brother. They used the crosswalk to join Cassie's family. "This is Afton. Afton, this is my father, Ben Clark, and my brother Darden."

"Nice to meet you, Afton," Cassie's father said. Both men were even better looking closer-up. Brother and sister could double as an ad for California tourism, they both just needed to be leaning against a couple of surfboards.

"Hi," Afton said to Cassie's father. Her attention was still on Afton's incredible looking brother. He had an amethyst set on a gold chain around his neck. This gorgeous guy was certainly comfortable with his masculinity to wear such a necklace, which was assuming anyone was foolish enough to bring it up.

"I want to take you to meet your father." That comment made by Cassie's father derailed her thoughts about Darden. "He wants to reconnect with you after all these years. I am sure you have many questions you want to ask him."

The pressure in Afton's head was back, worse than before, as well as an overwhelming desire to see her father. She had a lifetime of questions she wanted to address. Afton had often wondered about her father. Would he be like an aged Frank Langella? It was a pipe dream anyway, she had no idea how to cross from one universe to the next.

"How is it even possible?" she inquired.

"I am a crystal telepath," Cassie's brother replied. Afton had heard that term before; she just could not place where. "This crystal allows me to navigate dimensional portals. Your father sent us to bring you home." He held up the amethyst she had been admiring earlier.

"Home," Afton muttered. It was something she never had. She loved her grandmother, but this place had never felt right. When her grandmother passed away last summer, she was left alone in this world. Afton always knew she never belonged here. Would the life she had always dreamed about be possible with her father?

She had an affliction no one else seemed to have. Maybe there were other people like her in the other world. Would her constant feeling of isolation finally be coming to an end?

"Follow me and see for yourself," Darden said. He led her into a small grove of trees where three men awaited their arrival. They were as beautiful as Darden, which had not seemed possible when she first laid eyes on him. She looked back at him and noticed his amethyst was glowing. She had never seen a crystal do that. Afton followed Darden's gaze to an air displacement in front of them. "A portal to other parallel universes."

Afton approached the anomaly in wonder. "Universes?" She cautiously stuck her index finger into the dynamic air. She pulled it back and looked at it with curiosity. The finger seemed unaffected. A compulsion she did not understand was driving her to do something she only considered doing in the safe environment of dreams. To be honest, they were more nightmares than anything else.

"There are infinite multiple dimensions that exist," Darden answered. "Come with me to the Nightshade universe."

Afton took his hand and entered the portal. Had she realized the nightshade flower was deadly, maybe she would have given entering the portal a second thought.

Chapter 2

∽

The Nightshade Universe

Lorenz's fangs sunk into the throat of the woman who currently shared his bed. As always, he was careful not to break any of the delicate bones in her neck. He heard her cries of ecstasy as he fed from her. How easy it was to manipulate her mind into enjoying what was being done to her.

Her body writhed underneath him, as her legs rose to clasp around his hips. The smell of her arousal penetrated his nostrils. She was wet and ready for him. The problem was he had no desire to have sex with her, Lorenz only wanted her blood. For the life of him, he could not even remember her name.

He gorged until she lost consciousness. The volume of blood he took was not needed to feed his hungry cells. It would allow him to leave her without any fuss. Lorenz could glamour her desire for him away, but did not want to expend the energy to do even that.

Power soared through his body, although he felt empty inside. He rolled off the limp woman, rose from the bed, and dressed. Originally he planned to have sex with her as he fed, but his desire waned as a conversation he had prior to this interlude played over in his mind.

Yorik, the master of the Venture Hive, had summoned him. An agreement he had entered into eighteen years ago was finally going to be executed. To date, only Yorik was forced to abide by the terms of the treaty. Now, Lorenz was finally going to have to join with Yorik's half-ling daughter.

Lorenz's stomach turned with just the thought. Such creatures were an abomination. He had always imagined the girl would not live to see such a joining realized. When she had disappeared as a baby, he figured he was relieved of his side of the treaty that protected his people since its inception.

Lorenz maintained a small community not far from the Venture Hive. They had found a true synergy between the vampires and humans who lived and thrived here. The humans willingly provided their blood, while the vampires assured them a high quality of life.

Giving blood did not have to be an unpleasant experience. Lorenz turned and gazed at the woman on the bed. She was a regular donor, yet if you examined her body there were no telltale signs of her contributions. His people were always careful to heal the wounds they inflicted.

It was a crime in his community, not to mend the flesh that was torn during feeding. Failure to do so resulted in the vampire's eviction from Lorenz's home. Death of a human, accidental or not, would bring about the vampire's execution. Blood was too precious to lose even one human life.

After the donation, the donor was awarded a scrumptious feast. Food was abundant in the Nightshade universe, blood was not. He had secured the safety of his people by entering into a deal with Yorik. For almost two decades they had not been attacked by the master vampire's invincible forces.

He passed a mirror and looked at himself. Unlike most vampires, he was blond and had blue eyes. Since he had The Creator's blood in his veins, he appeared human. His fangs only elongated when he fed.

Lorenz found it humorous that the inhabitants of Ginkgo Terra, Earth, did not believe vampires cast a reflection. His kind had visited that parallel universe with the help of crystal telepaths. On Earth blood was plentiful, so much so, for a time they started speaking English in the Nightshade world.

However, it was not long before they discovered the mixture of oxygen to nitrogen in the Ginkgo Terra atmosphere actually caused their kind to slowly age. Due to that strange side-effect, very few vampires traveled there anymore.

The girl he was betrothed to grew up on Earth. She would return to the Nightshade universe with all kinds of misconceptions about his kind.

One weakness Ginkgo Terra folklore spoke of was true, vampires could not tolerate sunlight. The ultra-violet rays of the sun boiled their blood; they burned internally until all that was left was dust. To deal with this weakness to sunlight, canopies were placed over Nightshade settlements. The purple mesh made the sky appear violet. Underground rails connected settlements, allowing vampires to travel between hives with little risk.

Proximity to the sun weakened a vampire. It had been years since he had ventured outside, even knowing the protection of the tarp would protect him from the dangerous rays. Existing behind stone walls, his energy was unaffected whether it was night or day. A special treated glass was sometimes built into the stone to provide some natural light. That minimal defused light did not deplete his energy.

His mind kept reverting back to thoughts about the unfortunate girl he would have to take in. Her kind was a stain upon the world of vampires. A result of a mutated gene that created children who should never have been conceived, not to mention born.

In the old days, the women who carried the defected gene were destroyed as quickly as they were identified. The vampire and human races were not meant to be intermixed. After he had been made, he joined a society, The League, which helped to assure the purity of their blood. For two millennia, the group was visible and supported by vampire kind. It had only been in the last hundred years that The League was finally driven underground. As science advanced, it was believed the half-lings could be studied to determine how vampires could one day walk in the sun. It was the dream of every vampire to once again feel the warmth of sunshine on their faces without ill effect. Unfortunately, as their zeal to discover how to become day walkers increased, The League's practices became increasingly extreme. Now, their brotherhood was outlawed.

Once their activities were no longer condoned by the Vampire Council, The League became even more brutal. Their savagery made Lorenz re-think his involvement. When they originally started meeting in secret, Lorenz was still a member of the group. At that time he watched in horror as plans were developed to destroy a woman who was carrying a vampire's offspring. These plans, to torture the woman until she miscarried, followed by a gruesome death, were more than Lorenz could stomach. He paid a crystal telepath to assist him in rescuing the doomed woman and return her to the paternal vampire master.

Lorenz and the crystal telepath covertly entered the structure where the woman was being held. She had just been captured and her captors were waiting for the ruling elders of The League to arrive in order to witness the destruction of the child. Lorenz and his co-conspirator worked quickly.

The crystal telepath opened a portal from within the cell back to Yorik's hive. That was the first and last time he saw the woman who would bear the girl he was to join with. In an unforeseen development, though, the crystal telepath had fallen in love with the woman and later rescued her and her daughter. Lorenz had figured the woman's escape with her baby would end that chapter in his life. But he was wrong. Now the girl's reappearance would bring about complications Lorenz did not want to face.

Lorenz slid on a jacket and left the bed chamber. The rest of his home was frigid, only in his bedroom had a fire burned to heat its surroundings. His fortress had been built centuries ago as a means to protect his possessions against attack. In those days he held humans strictly for the blood they provided. The castle was built of stone with no concern for the comfort of his human cattle since vampires could regulate their body temperature against the elements.

He entered the main chamber and was surprised to see his blood brother, Drake, lounging in one of his chairs. Like Lorenz, his ancient blood allowed him to appear human, rather than the decaying corpses the other vampires of the Nightshade universe were slowly becoming. "I thought you were still at Yorik's stronghold," Lorenz said. Possessing the blood of The Creator made both Drake and Lorenz nobility among the vampire race. Drake traveled from hive to hive milking his status for all it was worth. Lorenz liked the stability of staying in one place.

"I was," his brother replied. "It dawned on me there was a possibility you are going to renege on your agreement with Yorik. Although I am hoping the men he sent to collect his daughter fail, you cannot afford to anger Yorik."

Lorenz's interest was piqued regarding why Drake hoped the mission to collect the girl failed. His brother had become as weary about continuing to live as he had. "What has gotten you so excited?"

"Not what," Drake answered, "but who. A lovely crystal telepath from the Troyk universe has fallen into my hands. She is being held hostage until Yorik's daughter is delivered to him. I naturally had to offer the beauty my protection." Lorenz could not remember a time his brother was not glib. It was one of the things he liked most about Drake.

"You do not stand a chance, brother," Lorenz said. "If he truly is her soul mate, no force of nature would divide those two. That includes you." He was intrigued by the look Drake threw him after his statement.

"I have been able to link into the soul mate channel that exists between them," Drake informed him. "If her mate does not deliver the girl, I merely need to continue romancing her as I have been doing." His brother leaned back further in the chair and placed his hands behind his head, cradling it. "Her blood is invigorating. I have not tasted anything like it in a very long time. She has sparked my desire to continue living."

Lorenz envied Drake for what he had found. Every century or so a vampire needed to become inspired by something or someone to desire to continue living. The boredom of eternity caused many vampires to willingly walk into the sun. Lorenz had worked hard over several millennia to find anything that would encourage him to go on. Now he had the half-ling to deal with. Would she be the catalyst to finally drive him into the light?

"Although I have tried to come up with a way to gracefully get myself out of the agreement with Yorik," Lorenz said. "I have been unable to do so. Until I have confirmed the girl has been brought before Yorik, I plan to continue to hold out for a miracle before I venture to his hive. It now appears we both have something to gain if those men are unsuccessful. You may bring your telepath here for her protection. There is no telling what Yorik will do when he realizes his daughter is lost to him."

"Either way," Drake countered, "I must return to Yorik's stronghold. Shirl has become an important part of my life and I do not want to leave her unprotected too long from Yorik. The master vampire has been playing with another woman from the Troyk universe. I am afraid once that woman dies, Yorik will cast his eyes on what I consider mine."

"Return here with your woman as soon it is clear the others have failed," Lorenz once again offered the invitation. He had already started to work on plans to reinforce the protection around his home. "Yorik would certainly think twice about attacking if two royal blooded vampires reside behind these walls."

"The time Yorik has given Shirl's brother and mate is running out," Drake said. "I must return to the Venture Hive. Word will be sent from Yorik if they are successful. My return with Shirl will indicate otherwise. Regardless, we will see each other soon. If they manage to bring the half-ling back, do not wait too long to come to see Yorik. He is ruthless when he feels he has been crossed. He may even do harm to his own child."

Drake stood and walked from the room. Their relationship was strong, forged through blood that was almost as old as time itself. They shared the same creator, although Drake was considerably older than Lorenz. So old, time had no measure. Lorenz wondered if he would live to be as old as his brother was now. Somehow he imagined the fate of the half-ling was the answer to that question.

Drake had never held the belief half-lings were unnatural. His blood brother believed in fairy tales, the ridiculous story about the joining of soul mates. Of all his brethren, Drake had taken the desertion of the master the hardest.

The stories that had developed in the master's wake were ridiculous. The tales told of how together, the male vampire and the female human would transcend into becoming a superior species. If the woman was a half-ling, it was believed the mating would produce an even more powerful bonding.

Lorenz had kept his involvement with The League from his brother. If Drake ever found out about what he had done in the past, Lorenz would not live to join with the half-ling. His blood brother would make sure of that.

Chapter 3

～

Afton was instantly cold, as she stepped into the Nightshade universe. A briskness came upon her, permeating her heavy jacket and jeans. She was literally chilled to the bone. Darkness and dampness were her first impressions of the world she was born in. Afton could barely see. But there was light in the distance, courtesy of some torches. The air she breathed was tainted with smoke. A shudder ran through her body, for some odd reason, she got the sensation she had walked over her own grave.

Her eyes quickly adjusted to the near absence of light. Afton always had incredible night vision, one of the few advantages of her strange affliction. There was nothing to see in these bleak surroundings. Perhaps if she turned around, she could get her bearing. However, her feet were glued in place. Defense mechanisms were being created by her body in reaction to this hostile environment.

Ice cold hands grabbed her arms and guided her into the embrace of a man. She looked up and saw a face she had often seen in her nightmares. Mercifully, she did not remember specifics about her dreams when she woke screaming. Now she was staring at the monster who plagued her nights and she knew this was no dream. Long repressed memories started flooding back into her conscious memory. Afton knew this creature was her father, she felt the familial bond between them.

Father or not, the man who held her looked like something straight out of a horror film. Under a black hood, his face was without any pigmentation. Terrible, dried up veins were exposed from under his transparent skin. His bloodshot eyes stood out, primarily because they glowed. Somehow she knew she was gazing at a blood crazed vampire. Without thought, she started to scream. She barely registered that the blood curdling cry came from within. Afton had no control over her reaction to what was holding her. This was not a fight or flight response, but one of pure terror. She was so petrified she could not move. What had possessed her to leave her safe haven?

Words spoken by a man behind her broke through her petrified state. They were spoken with such control. Since she was barely functioning, Afton had problems absorbing the words to make any sense of what was being discussed. What little she comprehended, she was being exchanged for another woman. In her confused state, she thought she heard the woman was a crystal telepath. Had she been a pawn in securing another woman's freedom?

Her father did not respond to the man who addressed him. He continued to pet her, as if she was a small dog or cat. At no point did her father speak to her. It felt like an eternity until soft, warm hands circled her upper arms. Someone was pulling her from the vampire's embrace.

Afton willingly stepped back and glanced around the room. Dozens of blood lusting vampires, with glowing eyes, stared back at her. Afton could not help it, she started to scream again. It was as if she were two women. One was taking in her surroundings and had the ability to reason, while the other was scared witless.

As she was dragged from the room, out of the corner of her eye she saw Darden. Struggling, she called out to him for help. He stood with the other men who had been with him earlier in the park. They did not even have the decency to look in her direction. Another pair of hands was placed around her waist, as she lost her battle to remain in the room. Why she even tried to stay with the men who had betrayed her was beyond her comprehension. She was all alone in this hellish world.

One of the vampires standing in the shadows watched as they dragged the abomination away. The girl's existence was why The League had existed for so long. These creatures continued to be produced regardless of how diligent they had become at killing the source, those women who had the genetic marker enabling them to successfully mate with the brethren.

Vampires were made, not born. Every child of such a union was born a half-ling, sick and weak. If such a child had been meant to live, it would have been strong and healthy. They did not belong in the world of vampires, even humans shunned them. These creatures belonged nowhere.

The girl had looked heartier than most of her kind. Very few grew to be the age she was now, The League made sure of that. She had been protected well wherever she had been taken when she was rescued as a child. He had to alert his brethren of her existence. Once again, they would have to deal with eliminating a being who never should have been born.

He could taste her blood already. The one consolation of killing such as her, the blood would be sweet. A delicacy beyond description. In his long life he had tasted only one half-ling child. He never forgot the ambrosia of the boy's life force. He would once again feast.

The vampire knew he had to keep his identity and purpose a secret. Yorik was too wrapped up with his new toy, and now his daughter, to know what was going on around him. He needed to plan his next steps carefully. It would not be long before he possessed the girl and her blood.

His cock stirred, as the juices in his mouth ran down his chin. He would satisfy one additional need before he watched the light leave her eyes. She would suffer as he had planned for her mother before she was snatched away. He knew Lorenz had been involved, but he had never been able to prove it. Once the turncoat took possession of his prize he would suffer! When he was done with Lorenz and the half-ling, no one would ever consider producing another unnatural child.

Afton was thrilled to be out of her father's presence. A shiver ran through her body as she remembered being held by him. It was an unnatural reaction for a child to have to her father, but there was nothing natural about his existence. For an instant when she saw Darden, she had dared to hope that he and his friends would rescue her.

As Afton and her escorts continued walking farther from the cave-like environment, her body started to warm. The stronghold was like a maze, as they made their way through a number of passageways. Windows had been carved into the stone, making her feel less claustrophobic. The purple light brightened their way, giving off a little heat. Afton figured the glass was tinted to protect the vampires.

Finally, they stopped in front of a double doored entry. Afton was surprised when they walked into a bedroom, rich with warm colors and light. Although there was no direct sunlight, the room was well lit with beautiful tiffany-like lamps. The beautiful stained glass shades must have contained every color in the rainbow. She imagined what Dorothy felt like after she arrived in Oz for the first time. Her mood automatically improved, as well as stabilizing her frayed nerves.

Her good temper quickly darkened as she finally got a good look at the women who had accompanied her. Their bodies were ravished by numerous unhealed vampire bites. There was more damaged skin than healthy. Afton was amazed they were even able to stand. One of the women walked up to Afton and extended her arm. When she did not react, the woman almost shoved her wrist into Afton's face.

"Drink," the woman demanded.

She must have seemed mentally impaired to the servant. Afton just stared, with her mouth open. They could not possibly expect her to drink their blood! She had always taken her nourishment from animals. Never had she considered drinking from a human. The very thought repulsed her.

"If you do not drink," the woman continued, "I will be punished by your father, Yorik." There was desperation in her voice Afton could not miss. Looking at the woman, she could not imagine how she could suffer any more than she already had. Afton's body once again shuddered at the thought.

"I do not drink from humans," Afton responded. "If you bring me animal blood that will be sufficient. I will tell whomever you fear that is my desire." She did not want to be the cause of any further injuries the woman suffered in this horrific place.

Afton watched a variety of expressions cross the woman's face as she considered her words. Would she trust her word if Afton was in the woman's position? She had been sorely abused in this stronghold or whatever her father's residence was called. Afton knew nothing of the world she had entered. Perhaps it was time to stop being the victim and start figuring out how things ran around here. Without that simple knowledge, she would never figure out how to leave this brutal world.

"What are your names?" Afton asked. The women first seemed surprised by the question. How were they directed if they were not addressed by name? Were they truly considered just cattle in this world? Her situation just kept getting better and better, Afton thought in despair.

"My name is Lenore," the woman who had asked her to drink her blood replied. "This is Shyrn," indicating to the woman who stood beside her. There was an awkward silence as both women exchanged a glance. It was obvious to Afton they did not know what to do next.

"Shryn, ask a servant to bring me animal blood," Afton requested. If she left the room, maybe Lenore would have the confidence to answer some of Afton's questions. There would be no one to witness the discussion. Shryn curtsied and quickly left the room.

Afton sat and indicated for Lenore to join her. Lenore looked around awkwardly before she joined her on the couch. "Tell me about this world," she ordered. Afton hoped she had put enough authority into her voice to intimidate Lenore into answering.

"What do you want to know?" Afton could barely hear the question, Lenore spoke so quietly. It was obvious she wanted to answer Afton's question without being overheard. The woman's eyes kept wandering, as if looking for a conspirator.

"Let's start by telling me where I am," Afton instructed.

"You are in the Nightshade universe," Lenore answered, her tone indicated she was surprised by the question. Lenore surveyed her surroundings before continuing. "There are multiple natural portals across this world where hapless people from other worlds fall through. I was born here. My mother often talked about the world she grew up in. There are worlds that exist that do not have these creatures." Her words had such longing, as if she was talking about mythical places.

"I come from Earth," Afton shared. "We do not have vampires either." She thought of all the vampire lore and wondered if people from the Nightshade universe had traveled to Earth. Afton needed to get back on track and continue to collect more information. "Are there places in this world where vampires do not reign?"

"No," Lenore shook her head, "but there are places where the two races live in harmony." Lenore shifted closer to Afton and whispered in her ear. "The vampire your father promised you to, runs a community where humans and vampires live side by side. People who share their blood are well rewarded and cared for. Will you take me with you when you join with him?" There was a desperate plea in Lenore's request.

Afton was so overwhelmed she did not answer. Her father married her off to another vampire? Would this day get any worse? Afton's rhetorical question was quickly answered as her father came storming into the room.

"What is the meaning of you asking for animal blood?" her father roared. If he was terrifying before, Afton could not find the words to describe how she felt now. She could barely control her body, she was shaking so badly. "Only the weakest of our kind stoop so low as to drink from common beasts, certainly not my own daughter. My people are starving and you have the nerve to ask for bestial blood!"

In the light her father looked more horrifying. What she thought was a colorless complexion was now tinted blue. Dried blood cells that scarred his face were responsible for the discoloration. Afton imagined his ravaged appearance was due to not getting enough blood. She almost felt sorry for her father.

When he spoke his sharp fangs were visible. They were both yellowed by age and reddened by the blood he had consumed from countless victims. Her tongue involuntarily ran over her eye teeth. Although they were the normal length for a human, in her nightmares they elongated, seeking blood.

Those feelings were short lived as he grabbed Lenore's wrist, forcing the woman to stand. Lenore cried out in pain, as her father almost took off the poor woman's hand. Yorik pulled the woman into his body and drew out a knife. He proceeded to cut a shallow slit into the woman's jugular. A red trail of blood slowly ran down Lenore's neck.

"You will drink or my blade will cut deep and she will not live. It is worth the sacrifice of her blood to teach you how to survive in my world." There was no mercy depicted in her father's face, only determination. Afton would not be the reason for Lenore's death.

She rose and took the few steps to stand before the bleeding woman. Afton tilted her head slightly and lapped up the blood, as a cat would cream. Her body immediately reacted to her first taste of human blood. She imagined it was like eating chocolate for the first time, magnified by a factor of fifty. Afton took Lenore in her arms and placed her lips around the wound, sucking up the blood. Using her breath, she suctioned more of the delicious liquid into her mouth. As the flow reduced to a trickle, Afton used what control she still possessed to prevent herself from biting the poor woman, and further opening the wound.

With the vivid thought of ripping the flesh around the cut, Afton was pulled from whatever spell she was under. She stepped back from Lenore, horrified at what she had just done. Without thought, she asked, "Is there a healing agent for her throat?"

Rather than getting an answer, her question was met with a slap across her face that sent Afton flying back onto the couch. The taste of her own blood now was co-mingled with the remnants of Lenore's. "These beings are of no consequence," her father bellowed. "You will learn your place in this world. I will not have you shame me by lowering yourself to care about what happens to these beings."

Her father's rant was interrupted by two of his guards entering the room. "Master," one of them said. "The Troyk men and women have escaped, including your new possession. Drake assisted them by holding back my men until they were all through the portal. I did not know a portal existed within the quarters where he had kept the female crystal telepath."

Afton did not know what the word berserk truly meant until her father reacted to the news. Yorik moved so quickly to the man's side who had just delivered the information, Afton merely witnessed a flash of movement. He literally ripped out the man's throat. Within a blink of an eye, her father did the same to the other guard. When he turned in her direction, his mouth and chin were covered with blood and the torn flesh from the dead vampires.

No longer able to hold back her body's reaction to what had occurred, Afton leaned forward and threw up the contents of her stomach. Afton and the carpet at her feet were covered in red bile. Her body continued to convulse helplessly with dry heaves.

Her inability to control her own constitution angered her father into a greater frenzy. He walked over and clasped one hand around her throat. Lifting her up, Afton frantically struggled to plant her feet on the ground, helpless in her father's grasp. He threw her a short distance into a nearby wall. Afton prayed the impact would kill her, allowing her to escape the nightmare her reality had become. To her horror, she was barely bruised. Lenora's blood must have made her body stronger to withstand such an attack.

"Clean her and this place up," her father ordered. "Make her presentable to sit by my side. I want Drake found and brought before me." Yorik exited the room without looking back.

Lenore made her way to where Afton lay on the floor and offered her hand. Afton could not handle the woman whose blood she drank assisting her. She slowly rose onto shaky feet, thinking she needed to shower and remove the regurgitation from her body. The last thing she wanted to do was follow her father's orders, but Afton could no longer stand the stench. She also needed to get away from the evidence of her deranged father's handiwork. Her eyes kept going back to the unfortunate vampires her father had killed. It was curious, there was so little blood.

Two women she had never seen before led her to the bathroom. They aided her in undressing and scrubbed her from head to toe. Afton could not bring herself to countermand her father's orders. For the time being she had no choice but to follow his dictates and not run the chance of displeasing him. Somehow, someway, she would find a way to break free of her father. The people who had brought her here had managed it. If it was the last thing she did, she would find a way.

Chapter 4

It had been a month since Afton had entered the Nightshade universe. Although she was now drinking human blood, for some reason it was not sustained her. The more she drank, the more she wanted. Regardless of how much she drank, she could not maintain her strength. Maybe the hormones they gave the animals on Earth were the reason she seemed healthier than she was now. Every day when she looked in the mirror her reflection startled her. She was wasting away a little each day. The white dresses she was forced to wear did not help to bring out what little pink she had left on her cheeks.

Her life had become a repetitive nightmare. One awful day bled into the next. A daily repeat of the dreadful experiences of the previous one. If her life went directly to DVD, it would be classified as horror, like *The Twilight Zone*. How she wished it had some type of a comedic edge to it, like *Groundhog's Day*. There was nothing humorous in what her life had become.

Every morning Afton was forced to sit beside her father as he held court. She hated this dark, cold, and miserable place, almost as much as she despised Yorik. The one consolation was she could barely see the vampires around her, only their glowing red eyes. None of them dared to approach her in Yorik's presence, which she was quite happy about. Yorik had her guarded twenty-four hours a day. He did not share why he appeared to be over zealous in his protection of her. The only harm she had sustained since arriving in this hell hole, had been at his hands.

Yorik continually switched the vampires who guarded her. Three of them had been executed before her very eyes, for failures, she had not been aware occurred. There had been no offensive actions toward her or even signs a threat existed. When her frayed nerves allowed, she examined the faces around her, looking for anything outside the norm. That turned out to be a waste of time. There was nothing normal about what her existence had become.

Although she was surrounded by vampires and servants, she had never felt more alone in her life. She was an oddity here, as much as she was on Earth. At least back home, she was not exposed to homicidal rampages. Afton could not ignore the looks she was given, ranging from pity to outright hatred. To make matters worse, Lenore had disappeared. Afton did not know if she had been reassigned or executed for talking to her. Every time she tried to talk to someone they left her presence - she had not spoken for days.

While she was ruminating about her current situation, a flash of light to her right caught her eye. She watched four people exit what she assumed was the portal she had originally come through. Her declining eyes also made out that two men and two women had entered their world.

"Drake has given me and my companions safe passage in this world," the tall blond woman among the new arrivals announced. Afton remembered that Drake was the vampire who had aided in the escape of several Troyk citizens when she first arrived. The traitor vampire had left her father's fortress before he was captured. Interestingly enough, she had heard rumors that he had escaped to the community where her future husband ruled.

Although Yorik had been incensed when Drake had helped his prisoners escape, he had eventually pardoned him upon learning the vampire had allied himself with Lorenz. Her father had expected Lorenz to arrive immediately upon having been summoned to the Venture Hive. His kinship with Drake had delayed his arrival, pending his blood brother's improved standing in Yorik's court. It appeared her father wanted to make peace with her yet to be seen intended, more than he wanted Drake destroyed.

Her father sat up straighter on his throne. "New blood is always welcome," he said in an eerily friendly voice. Afton braced herself, preparing for the vampires to tear these people from limb to limb. Having seen such violence in the last month, she had almost become desensitized to it.

The blond woman turned around and seemed shaken by Afton's presence. She was absolutely stunning. Afton immediately recognized the two men as those who had accompanied Darden when she was brought across to this universe. A small woman with light auburn hair was also with them.

The tall woman got control of herself. "I have come to see Drake," she adjusted her posture after she said those words. Afton imagined she wanted to seem stronger than she was. "Blood will be awarded to those who assist me. However, Drake must captain the Nightshade contingent on this campaign."

Her father's attention must have been piqued as he leaned forward. "Perhaps a down payment is called for." The woman seemed temporarily shaken. That certainly was not an unexpected reaction. The two men moved to stand in front of the two women. Having seen her father in action, their posturing would not save them if her father wished to do harm.

She watched her father rise slowly and walk before the man protecting the short redhead. "Your mate is with child," her father addressed the man with short black hair. "A true blessing. Please come forward, my sweetheart."

Afton watched in fascination as the diminutive woman placed her hand on the back of the man who stood in front of her. He stepped aside as she came forward. Her father and the woman stared at each other, captivated. She had never heard her father speak so lovingly to anyone. Afton had not thought it possible.

"A special child you carry," her father said. "You must bring her back to this world when she is of age. Nightshade is her destiny." Afton cried out internally for the woman not to listen to her father. She needed to keep her child safe, free of this terrible place.

"I don't think so," the little woman replied. "Never in a million years would I subject my daughter to the horror you have exposed your child to." Afton stiffened in her chair. How could this woman possibly know who she was? It then dawned on her that the tall blond was the crystal telepath who had escaped from this world, the one held captive in exchange for her. Afton honestly did not know how she felt about that discovery.

What happened next surprised Afton, but this whole discussion had been full of surprises. Her father actually laughed. She had never heard anything but anger in his voice. "You have fire, my girl," Yorik said. "It is too bad you found your soul mate. My little sprite, you would have given me years of entertainment and blood."

The black haired man, her father called the redhead's mate, moved back in front of the woman. She was probably only a couple years older than Afton. She also saw the blonde changing her stature to a more aggressive stance.

"Relax, my Troyk warriors," her father said. "No one is safer in my realm than this little girl, and Shirl is under Drake's protection. He should be here within the hour. In the meantime, let me introduce you to my daughter, Afton."

She almost missed the introduction, since she was momentarily preoccupied by the fact Drake would be coming. Maybe the man she was given to would be with him. Afton stepped forward, not daring to say a word. She was afraid her voice would shake.

"I will be happy to return Afton home," the one her father called Shirl said. Afton turned to the woman, but held her tongue. "Her friends must be frantic by now. She is a child of light. Her aura is dimming with all this darkness." Although Afton did not believe in all the new age nonsense, she did not doubt what Shirl said was true. Daily she saw evidence of her deteriorating body. Fearing to hope her father would take up Shirl's invitation, Afton momentarily held her breath.

It did not take long for her father to destroy any dream she had of leaving Nightshade. "This is her home now," Yorik answered. "However, I can make sure she is exposed to sunshine. Her intended is arriving with Drake. Your timing is really quite remarkable." Afton struggled to hide her surprise and excitement. Lorenz was finally coming.

More words were exchanged between her father and their visitors, but they were lost on her. Afton was so overcome by the news that Lorenz would be here soon, she spaced out through a portion of the discussion. Nightly she dreamed of him coming to save her from the living nightmare she lived every day in her father's realm. She knew he would be different from the monsters within her father's hive. A knight in shining armor would certainly be welcome at this point.

"Powerful enough to remedy a kidnapping that should never have occurred." Shirl's words pulled her out of the daydream she was having related to Lorenz. This brave woman certainly had a death wish.

Afton looked back and forth between her father and Shirl. It was like a sick game of chicken that could possibly end in a pool of blood. Afton sat and grabbed the sides of her chair with each hand. She could feel her nails digging into the wood.

"I am her only family," her father finally ended the silence. "She represents the mortality of my bloodline. Do you really believe I could do her harm?" Her father never shared this with her. Afton did not know if he was genuine or grandstanding against a woman who held unknown telepathic gifts. Shirl kept staring at Afton as if she had all the answers.

The little redhead once again came forward. "As far as I can see, your daughter appears to be petrified. She is too afraid to voice her own wishes." Afton paled at those words. She had forgotten about the pregnant Troyk woman who had somehow blended into the shadows.

Afton did not know what powers Shirl possessed, she just knew she could not have their deaths on her conscience. "I wish to stay," Afton managed to get out in a voice no more than a whisper.

The redhead approached her. "This may be your last chance to go home. My name is Alex. I found myself in a parallel world after I was dragged through the portal. It was terrifying, but I was surrounded by people who cared for and ultimately loved me. I want nothing less for you. My soul mate was one of the men who brought you here. Please, let us make things right."

Afton was touched by her words. If she did nothing else in this life, she was going to save this wonderful woman. She lied to end this conversation and guarantee Alex's safety. "I am of his blood. Things were never right on Earth. Maybe I will find a place here to belong."

She had told the truth about her feelings related to Earth. It could never be her home again. The only thing she knew about her future in the Nightshade universe was that it would be short and she would die violently.

The vampire lurking in the shadows did not know whether he was pleased or disappointed when Yorik would not allow the Troyk crystal telepath to return the abomination to her previous home. On several occasions he tried to get close to the girl, but had been unsuccessful in each attempt. Yorik had her guarded as if she was a rare gem. He did not understand the master's obsession with the girl. Most of the time he treated her with indifference.

Since she had arrived in the Nightshade universe, the girl had started to waste away. If he did not take action soon, there would not be much of her left to enjoy. Each day when she joined her father on the dais, he envisioned all the ways he would violate her. His body came alive as it had not for centuries when he imagined himself driving into her.

He would have to find an opportunity to sweep her away before Lorenz and his contingent made it impossible. Perhaps he was being too hasty. Hedging his chances of success, he knew he had to come up with other locations where he could execute his plans. Perhaps when Lorenz shepherded her to his property. There would be opportunities in the tunnels to abscond with her before Lorenz could gather more of his forces.

In the meantime, he would watch and listen. The more intelligence he could gather, the better his chances were to grab the girl. There was no doubt she would be his, the only question was how soon.

Chapter 5

~

Dread consumed Lorenz as he walked through the endless corridors of the Venture Hive. He had postponed his trip to meet Yorik's half-ling for as long as he could. Between the unfortunate deal he brokered eighteen years ago and the mess Drake had gotten himself into with Yorik, he had no choice but to visit this dreadful place.

It was hard to overlook the mistreatment of the humans who lived within the walls of the compound. Violence was evident on the bodies of most of the servants he came across. Centuries ago he had victimized his sustenance in such a manner, something that still shamed him.

"You are quiet," Drake commented as they were led to meet the girl Lorenz would join with. "Let us get this over with so I can meet with my crystal telepath. Yorik has demanded we spend time with his daughter before I get my just reward to be reunited with Shirl."

"Convenient how you have overlooked she has her soul mate with her," Lorenz chuckled at his blood brother. He was in a foul mood and Drake was an easy target to vent his frustrations upon. If he continually reminded himself of the peace his settlement has known for the last eighteen years, perhaps the price he has now paid would not continue to get underneath his skin.

"Wait until you meet the vision of my life, then you will not be so quick to judge my feelings for her," Drake replied. Lorenz glanced at his brother and saw pure joy written over his face. He envied the short bit of happiness Drake had been able to buy himself.

However, Lorenz was a realist and knew Drake would soon be suffering from the loss of his crystal telepath. She wanted something from Drake, but not to be with him. There lay the issue. Perhaps in comforting his blood brother, Lorenz's own plight would be lessened.

The servant they were following stopped and knocked on the door she stood before. A muffled voice came from the other side and the woman opened the wood door. Lorenz's reprieve from the agreement he made with Yorik had now officially ended, he entered the room to meet the abomination he was tied to, perhaps for life.

Lorenz was partially blinded by the light, colorful room. Vampires were not sensitive to artificial light, they just surrounded themselves with near darkness and somber colors. The brightness of the room just shocked his senses. However, it was the woman who stood before him that brought him to a sudden stop.

What he saw was a vision of what the wan, dreadfully skinny woman could become. There was no mistaking the woman draped in white was a half-ling, the intelligence he provided had been responsible for the disposing of many of them over the years. Lorenz was still haunted by his misguided actions in the past.

Afton was different than the ones who came before her. He could see a vibrant, beautiful woman under the sickly, pale near skeleton before him. The joining would make his vision a reality.

"Outrageous," Drake muttered beside him. His blood brother surged forward, bit his wrist, and shoved it into Afton's mouth. "Drink! How Yorik allowed you to waste away in this fashion is beyond me."

She first seemed taken aback by Drake's sudden action. Ultimately, Afton did not fight Drake, she willingly drank his blood. Euphoria was written over her face, as she continued to enjoy the ancient, powerful life force Drake offered her. A momentary feeling of jealousy washed over Lorenz, before he decided it was ridiculous and pushed the emotion from his consciousness. Not only was he seeing things, he was reacting in a very unusual manner.

Realizing Afton had taken as much of Drake's blood as she needed, his brother released the girl. Her eyes had wandered over to him from time to time, but Lorenz stood mute. He had never had any issues communicating, but this woman had the oddest effect on him. For the first time in his existence, he was not sure how to approach a woman he desired.

"Are you Lorenz?" Afton asked Drake, her eyes yet again stealing a glimpse of Lorenz before returning to the vampire she addressed. The girl seemed at ease with his friend, even though he seemed to draw her attention. Lorenz wondered what her reaction would be when she realized he was the man she sought.

"My name is Drake," his brother said, taking her hand and kissing it. Charmed oozed from the bastard, Lorenz wanted to beat the stupid smile from his face. She was not his to seduce, but Lorenz's. He was once again taken aback by his reaction to the half-ling.

"My father is not very happy with you," Afton laughed. Her voice was light and lovely, as she would be one day. "You have visitors that wish your assistance, they just-" Afton stopped speaking and looked in Lorenz's direction, panic in her eyes.

It felt like time stood still as Lorenz struggled to find the right words to address the woman he would be joining with. Where she was at ease with Drake, it appeared she was panicking when she realized who he was. Awkward did not begin to describe how the situation felt. He had never been tongue-tied in his life.

"I believe the Earth has an expression about dumb blondes?" Drake said. "This one is Lorenz. If you will excuse me, I have a beautiful one waiting to speak with me." Drake came up beside him and spoke quietly. "Join me after you get your senses back. I may need your assistance for the time being."

Lorenz watched Drake leave the room, not replying to his final request. He turned around just in time to see Afton falter. Shaken out of his ineptitude, Lorenz rushed over to the girl.

Afton grabbed the chair she stood before, as the room started to spin. Strong, capable hands grabbed her as her legs gave out underneath her. She felt too crappy to appreciate that the most beautiful man she had ever laid eyes on held her in his arms. Feelings of embarrassment quickly changed to mortification when she realized she was going to vomit the blood Drake had given her.

Lorenz masterfully brought her down to her knees and placed a large bowl before her, obviously aware of what was about to happen. He held back her hair as she emptied her stomach. From what she understood about Drake, he was almost as old as time and the blood was probably too rich for her constitution. It had been the best thing she had ever tasted. She became more aware of Lorenz next to her as the convulsions ended. Like Drake, he did not look like a vampire. Lorenz certainly had not acted like one, aiding her while she was sick was a very sweet thing to do.

"Let us get you up and refreshed," Lorenz said. He helped her to the bathroom where she proceeded to brush her teeth and wash her face. Lorenz left her temporarily, probably having the evidence of her illness removed. After the third time scrubbing her teeth, she was ready to return to the comfort of her bed. When he returned, Lorenz lifted and carried her out of the bathroom. Again she was struck by how kind he was, nothing like the other vampires who hovered around her father.

"Thank you," she feebly uttered, as he placed her on the soft mattress. "You should join Drake and see what aid you can provide." Afton could not rest until Alex was no longer in the Nightshade universe. They had not confided in her father what they wanted, but she felt it must be something critically important for them to reenter this bleak, deadly world.

"If he needs me, he knows where to find me," Lorenz replied. "What have you been eating since you have been here? You look dreadful."

Boy, he certainly did not hold back punches, Afton thought. "Human blood," she answered, casting her eyes down. Where he had criticized how she looked, Afton could only see beauty when she looked at him. His blond hair was a perfect complement to his pale complexion. He looked more like a Hollywood vampire, than the blood-lusting vampires that lived within her father's hive. She did not understand how this world worked. Drake and Lorenz looked wonderful, while all the other vampires she had encountered had frightening appearances.

"Were you this sickly in Ginkgo Terra?" Lorenz inquired. At the puzzled look on her face, he modified his question. "What did you eat or drink when you lived on Earth?"

"I cannot tolerate food," she replied. "Back home, I drank animal blood, anything the butcher had handy. The animals on Earth are given different drugs to fatten them up. I imagine the hormones and antibiotics they received had a better effect on me than the blood I have been forced to drink here."

Silence followed the explanation of her diet. She wanted to ask him questions about his life and when he would rescue her from the terrors of her father's hive. Helpless, she just lay there, waiting for any response from him. Her eyes continued to soak in his beauty.

"I should see what the Troyk contingent wants," Lorenz finally said. She felt a loss when he started to leave. "They have a crystal telepath with them. Part of my fee in assisting them will be animal blood from Earth."

"My father will not allow me to drink such blood," she said before she thought about his reaction. The violence her father inflicted at her request, was still at the forefront of her mind.

"It no longer matters what your father thinks or does," he responded. "You are my responsibility now, regardless of where you currently reside. I do not imagine this will take long." Her heart sank as he turned to leave and closed the door behind him. She immediately felt the loss of his presence.

Afton readjusted the pillows and closed her eyes. Regardless of her dreams, she had feared the type of monster her father was giving her to. Relief warmed her as she played back her first encounter with her future husband. There would be no ceremony as there was on Earth, but she could not help but think of him in such terms. Although she could not explain it in words, Afton already felt a bond between her and Lorenz.

Perhaps she would finally have a decent night's sleep, free of the nightmares that continued to plague her rest. Could she dare hope that she had her happily ever after, or would the inherent horrors of the Nightshade universe swallow any happiness she could possibly find with Lorenz?

Lorenz was once again following a servant through the maze of the Venture Hive. The reaction he had to Afton still surprised him. Feelings he never possessed before were playing with his ability to maintain control.

He cared for the people who lived in his community, but feelings of cherishing and tenderness had never existed until he laid eyes on Afton. Balancing the warm emotions was almost a crippling fear related to her well-being. He had a lot to consider. Lorenz knew better than most what her being a half-ling meant, and the target she represented to his former brethren within The League.

He almost regretted leaving the group, since he did not know if any of their members resided in Yorik's hive. The master vampire had communicated to him the security he had placed around his daughter, fearing The League would go after her. He planned to supplement Yorik's security with his own now that he had met Afton. He already knew he could not bear anything happening to the girl.

They reached their destination and the servant communicated that Drake was currently in an outer garden with one of the Troyk citizens. It did not take much effort for Lorenz to figure out which member of their team his blood brother was with. Under normal circumstances, he would not have deprived Drake of his time with Shirl, but Lorenz was anxious about leaving Afton alone.

He leaned against the stone wall, making plans for Afton's evacuation from this hive, when Drake and a tall blond woman arrived. She was certainly everything Drake said she would be, absolutely beautiful. However, a vibrant black haired woman with chocolate brown eyes kept entering his mind.

Drake, Shirl, and Lorenz joined the group assembled. In the customary manner, he greeted Drake's crystal telepath with a kiss on her hand. Desiring to be back with Afton, he pushed along the discussion by asking, "What is it you wish from Drake?"

The female crystal telepath requested their aid in rescuing her friend and another member's brother from the Troyk penal colony. Only half-listening to the discussion, Lorenz struggled with how he was going to transform the sickly Afton into the vision he kept seeing when he looked at her. Based on the condition she was currently in, he knew he had to act fast.

Her inability to digest Drake's blood presented an issue he had not foreseen. If she reacted to his brother's blood in that fashion, his life-force would create the same issue. The girl's health had to be improved before he could consider joining with her. He glanced at Drake as he pondered the question of how to save Afton.

Odd was a good description of the look on Drake's face. His brother's focus seemed to leave the blond crystal telepath and was now focused on the little redhead. Lorenz had sensed she was pregnant, but Drake seemed almost obsessed with the prospect.

Pulling his friend aside, he asked, "What is wrong with you?" In the thousands of years he had known Drake, he had never seen him like this.

"*The child spoke to me,*" Drake confessed telepathically. Although vampires could communicate in this fashion among blood brothers, they rarely did. It further emphasized the magnitude of Drake's new obsession.

"*Impossible,*" Lorenz responded in the same fashion. "*I recognize the unborn female will carry the genetic marker, but a child within the womb cannot communicate telepathically.*"

"*She is special,*" Drake continued. "*The baby does not communicate in words, but in emotions. Her parents are soul mates and she knows of the soul union between a human and a vampire.*"

Lorenz knew his friend was reading too much into whatever he was picking up from the chameleon's child. The redhead had an uncanny ability to blend into the background. He approached the father of the child. "I will join Drake to free your brother," Lorenz told the man. "Ties of blood are important among the kindred. Two of our elite guards will join us and protect your mate. Nothing is more precious than your daughter."

The baby's father, Tarsea, thanked him and moved next to his soul mate. No doubt, he was as troubled with Drake's attention toward his mate as Lorenz was. He had two more things he needed to do before a portal was opened for their rescue mission. Lorenz walked up to Shirl and her soul mate, Starc. It was not hard to miss that the woman had her eyes glued on Drake, who in turn was looking at Alex. Shirl knew what it meant to be the subject of his blood brother's obsession.

"I have a personal request," Lorenz addressed Shirl. "Yorik's daughter Afton is now under my protection. I need animal blood laced with antibiotics and hormones to feed the girl. If she does not receive the blood soon, she will become a living skeleton."

"Let me return her to Earth," Shirl said with conviction. "This is a miserable, terrible place. I still have nightmares about everything I saw and experienced here."

Lorenz quickly shook his head. The idea of returning her to Ginkgo Terra was not acceptable. Afton was his and Lorenz would do whatever it took to keep her. "The girl drinks blood, she does not belong on Earth. There are places within the Nightshade universe that are very different than this foul stronghold. I plan to take her to such a place as soon as I can pry her from her father's side."

The blonde stared long and hard at Lorenz. He must have passed muster because she nodded her head in agreement. Lorenz had one more item to address before the crystal telepath opened the portal. Lorenz tracked down a servant to lead the six elite guards he brought with him from his community to this room. Two would travel with him and protect Alex, while four stayed behind and would watch over Afton.

Metal armor was delivered for the vampires to wear. Piercing a vampire's heart would also cause him to internally combust. The battle wear also had a high neckline, protecting them from decapitation. No creature, not even a vampire, could survive their head being severed from their body. A vampire's incredible strength allowed him to wear his protective gear with little ill-effect. Lorenz had every intention of returning from this little skirmish. For the first time in eons, he had a reason to live.

He watched in wonder as a portal opened. The Creator would manipulate energy when they traveled from world to world. It looked very different than the air displacement before him. Lorenz had never left the Nightshade universe once they called this world their home.

It had also been decades since he fought in battle. He could feel the adrenaline in his blood soaring through his veins. The primeval make-up of every vampire longed for the rush of devouring the life-force of a defeated enemy during battle. Lorenz would fight on this day, but longed instead to taste the blood of members of The League who would do harm to Afton. He just needed to fight this one battle quickly and return to his woman before a member of The League could get their hands on her.

Chapter 6

~

Afton stared at the ceiling, too pumped up to sleep. So many things were rushing through her brain, she had problems completing one thought when another one came out of nowhere to gather her attention. Her brain would not shut up, making it impossible for her to consider getting any rest.

Image after image of what her future husband would look like had dominated her thoughts since she had arrived in the Nightshade universe. One as bad as the next kept her up at night. Her nightmares were fueled by the creatures she was subjected to during the day.

When she saw Drake, a sense of relief had washed over her. To discover the incredible looking blond behind him was to be her husband overwhelmed her. Lorenz was the ideal man she had dreamed of most of her life, but never dared to hope she would end up with something this spectacular. Even his wavy blond hair had been right on point.

Frustrated, she could not sleep, Afton pushed back the covers. Perhaps a brisk walk through the maze of hallways would burn off some of her excess energy. It would probably be hours before Lorenz and Drake returned.

Warmth spread through her body as she thought of Lorenz. Would he come to her as soon as he returned from assisting the Troyk warriors? If she got a little exercise, maybe she would get some color in her cheeks. He certainly did not look at her as if she were wasting away, although he had been blunt in his communication to her about her appearance. There was a note of concern in his voice, not censure.

She quickly dressed and was met by six guards when she opened the bedroom door. The four new guards identified themselves as Lorenz's personal guard. They were to accompany her anywhere she went outside the safety of her private rooms. Their presence reconfirmed her impression that Lorenz cared for her.

Not sure of her destination, Afton started walking aimlessly through the endless corridors of her father's stronghold. She did not care where she ended up, as long as it was not the receiving hall where her father held court. Yorik was the last person she wanted to run into.

As they entered a section of the palace she had never been in, an elderly woman came up to her. Lorenz's guards stopped the servant before she reached Afton. The woman seemed harmless enough, she was human, after all. Other humans had shied away from her, while this woman initiated contact. Afton motioned to the guards she would speak with the woman.

"Why did you return?" the woman said accusingly. "Your mother sacrificed everything for you."

Afton was taken aback. Had this woman known her mother? The thought that anyone could survive this hell hole for the eighteen years she had been gone seemed incredible.

"People of the Troyk universe exchanged me for one of their own," Afton informed the woman. Why she was explaining herself was lost on her.

"Well, that explains it," the woman answered. "Must have been a mind control telepath who lured you here. They can fill your mind with what they want you to do and make you believe it was all your idea. Did you feel pressure in your head when you were with them? That is what it feels like when they manipulate your brain. I have met several of them in my life."

Afton remembered the headaches she experienced first with Cassie and then with Ben Clark. They had convinced her she wanted to see her father. She had been tricked into coming here and now Lorenz was helping to rescue two of their friends. Anger would do her no good at this point. This woman had known her mother and could fill in the gaps her grandmother had been unable to provide.

"Tell me about my mother," Afton asked the woman. She hungered for information on how her mother had survived and eventually escaped this world.

"She was a beautiful woman who had been ill used by Yorik," the woman said. The woman was fearless speaking thus in her father's stronghold.

"When he realized she carried the genetic marker that would allow her to breed with him, your father took his assaults to a new level. He was going to get her pregnant one way or another. Every month when her period came, she was punished for not conceiving. She cried in my arms after every beating."

Mercifully, the woman stopped talking due to her sobs. Afton was having problems holding back her own tears. She barely remembered her mother. It was as if they were talking about another person altogether. How would she ever be able to sit in the same room as her sadistic father? If she had said the words out loud, she could have choked on the last word.

"What is your name?" Afton asked, taking the woman in her arms.

"Beryth, my lady, I served your mother and then cared for you after your birth." Beryth took her hand and ran it lightly against Afton's cheek. Nana had done the same affectionate touch when she was little. "You were such a sickly baby. Despite everything that had happened to her, your mother loved you dearly."

Afton heard footsteps coming in their direction. From the sound, there was a small army not far from where they stood. "Go now," Afton commanded. "I will find you later." She watched as the woman scurried away.

Within a matter of moments her father and eight of his guards were on top of them. Afton did not like the expression on her father's face. She turned to make sure Beryth was not in sight.

"You were not in your rooms," her father said accusingly. He had not visited her since that disastrous first day.

"I wanted to get some exercise before Lorenz returned," Afton told her father. She tried not to have any edge in her voice. It was difficult to address her father in a civil tone after the latest atrocity she learned Yorik had been guilty of.

With a critical eye, her father inspected the guards Lorenz had left behind. He nodded to them, she suspected, giving his approval of the job they were doing.

"Be prepared to receive Lorenz when he returns from war," her father ordered. "You will partake in drinking the blood of our fallen enemy. Do not embarrass me by declining the blood. He has informed me that you are now under his guardianship. Regardless of what man you are with, you will always be of my blood. Do not forget that."

Her father left, but not before giving her a look that sent shivers down her spine. She only hoped that Beryth would not disappear as Lenore had. Reluctantly she followed in the wake of her father.

Chapter 7

~

The Troyk Penal Colony

Lorenz was frustrated with all the waiting they were forced to do since exiting the portal. They entered a nearly deserted encampment, only to find the lone inhabitant hysterical once she spotted them. She had been a captive along with the female crystal telepath in the Nightshade universe. Unlike Shirl, the woman Chartail had not been under Drake's protection. Yorik had abused her and it took Alex to calm her down, assuring her the vampires meant her no harm.

All in all, they presented an adequate fighting body. The Troyk men had supplemented their number with the warriors from Terra Nova. Lorenz had never visited that world, but from the looks of them, they knew how to fight. They were ready. They just needed an enemy to conquer. He worked hard to contain the feral vampire who existed deep inside of him, the one that wanted the blood promised.

After she had calmed Chartail, Alex was able to learn the men who lived in this village had gone to attack the community where the people they had come to rescue resided. It looked like they were going to get their share of blood and then some. Lorenz hoped the battle would take his mind off worrying about Afton. She had seldom left his thoughts, since he left the Nightshade universe.

As they walked to the neighboring village, Drake walked along beside Alex. Her soul mate foolishly led the charge, leaving her behind. Although she was a little thing, Alex showed no fear being surrounded by vampires. She explained she had been pulled through the portal while hiking in Ginkgo Terra. The way she figured, if she could survive having Tarsea as a soul mate, she could handle anything.

Lorenz got the impression he was a little overprotective of his soul mate. Listening to Alex talk, Lorenz could understand why. The girl had no common sense in his opinion. She seemed oblivious to Drake's interest in her unborn daughter. He debated whether he should have a conversation with the child's father. Drake's new obsession with the baby placed both the mother and the little girl in peril.

They were nearing the gorge which provided a natural barrier between the enemy and the encampment. The portal guardians, as Shirl referred to them, had taken part of their forces and took the long way around the gorge to attack the Utopia settlement before a second force came across the canyon. From his vantage point, it appeared the village was on fire and the battle was close to over. They had arrived just in time.

The Terra Nova warriors with their broad swords made mincemeat of the force still crossing the bridge to finish off the villagers. The Nightshade vampires followed, grabbing any of the enemy who were not already down. Lorenz held back, waiting for the right person to attack.

He entered the village, which was engulfed in smoke. However, even though the stink of the fire's aftermath, he could smell the insanity coming off a woman about to attack a wounded, female warrior. Fortunately, insanity did not taint the blood, only the mind. Lorenz no longer liked to kill, but if it was a mercy killing or a freeing of a troubled soul, he had less of a problem with it.

With the stealth of an animal, his soon-to-be victim attacked the fallen warrior woman. Lorenz swept down on the insane predator and sunk his fangs into her neck. Unlike taking blood from a willing donor, Lorenz was not careful, breaking the delicate bones in the mad woman's neck.

Her blood was sweet, free of what had driven her insane. When he was done with her, he discarded her body. It was now a hollow shell, deserving no special treatment. The blood had fed his hungry cells and strengthened him to continue fighting.

The warrior woman he had saved had a knife embedded in her shoulder. Lorenz left her in Alex's care before the blood seeping from the wound attracted his primal beast. The girl was one of the Troyk citizens they had come to rescue.

The next body he took was a man with a long jagged scar on his face. He refused to surrender, so Lorenz took his blood and drank until the enemy was dead. Like Yorik, this man victimized women. He read the man's mind, as his victim drew his last breaths of air. An appropriate death for a dishonorable man.

It did not take long for the opposition to surrender. They did not stand a chance against the vampires and the force they supported. The only thing left was to determine what to do with the prisoners.

Drake remarked to the Troyk men that delivering the enemy to Yorik would mend relations between their peoples. The vampires needed the crystal telepathic assistance in traveling between worlds and the Troyk government needed the crystals they mined in the Nightshade universe. There was a nice synergy in the relationship they had built to date, it would have been foolish not to take steps to strengthen their bonds.

They met in the center of the village. By some miracle their largest hut had escaped damage. The children had been gathered and protected in that location. Survivors of the battle were now comforting the children and shielding them from the aftermath of what had occurred.

Another of the Troyk citizens they had come to rescue was among them. Lorenz sensed the close relationship the young man had with the kids. He studied the sensitive manner in the way he addressed them. Lorenz felt he needed to emulate this style for when he dealt with Afton.

An older man who fought alongside them approached him and Drake. He appeared to have the weight of the world on his shoulders. Where the others were shying away from the vampires, it intrigued Lorenz that this man had sought them out.

"My name is Benko Jarlyn," the man introduced himself. "Jeryl Jarlyn, my father, is the Prime Ruler of the Troyk universe. It is my intention to one day overthrow him and rule in his stead. He supplied you blood in exchange for crystals. I wish to enter negotiations for those crystals. It is also my intention to destroy the master of the Venture Hive for his role in victimizing my soul mate, Chartail."

Not surprising to Lorenz, Drake stepped forward. "The crystals are yours. I will also assist you in bringing down Yorik. Any blood would be appreciated, but not required. What I desire is access to the pregnant woman Alexandra and ultimately her daughter."

Lorenz could see Benko was taken aback by Drake's demand. No future leader in his right mind would agree to Drake's ridiculous terms. The question was how desperate Benko Jarlyn was for their crystals.

"That will not be possible," Benko finally said.

"That is my price," Drake answered. "It is asking very little compared to what you will be gaining. I mean the girl and her child no harm. The baby has already contacted me telepathically. Being from a telepathic race yourself, I am sure you understand the significance of that."

Once again, Benko seemed dumbstruck by what came out of Drake's mouth. Lorenz could see the internal struggle the future Troyk ruler had with Drake's requirement. In the end, he merely nodded.

"I will talk to her soul mate," Benko responded. "It will not be an easy discussion, but I will see what I can do. There is one other thing I would like. I was involved in getting a woman from Earth, Ginkgo Terra, to enter the Nightshade universe. This same Yorik held one of ours in exchange for his daughter. I would like the girl returned to her home on Earth."

Lorenz barely gave Benko the time to finish his sentence. "That will not be possible. The girl is now mine. She will come to no harm under my protection." He now knew the frustration Drake must have felt when another held the strings to his happiness.

"She is a young woman who should not be living with vampires," Benko said. Although he planned to fight Benko, Lorenz could not help but to respect the man. He took responsibility for what he did and tried to rectify the mistake he made.

"The girl requires blood to live," Lorenz countered. "I will do my best to find a place within the Nightshade universe where she will be happy."

Benko Jarlyn stared at Lorenz for several moments, determining his trust-worthiness. This was one argument the future ruler of the Troyk universe was not going to win. Besides, Lorenz had time on his side, an advantage of being immortal.

"If I can see the girl from time to time, to make sure she is being taken care of, you have yourself a deal," Benko ended the negotiations.

There was no more to be done. The prisoners who survived the battle would all be accompanying the vampires back to the Nightshade universe. It was the only way the villagers would be able to live in peace, with no fear of reprisals once they left. Yorik would have his blood in the short term.

They walked back to the portal guardian village, where the vampires had originally entered this universe. The female crystal telepath opened the portal and the prisoners were herded through with Yorik's men. Lorenz held back, not sure what type of reception he would get from Afton. He had been given the opportunity to return her to Earth, a means to be free of a relationship he never wanted.

The image of the woman she would one day morph into, kept entering his mind. He could not deny the attraction he had for her right from the start. Could he face her and not admit he had the opportunity to free her and he turned it down for his own selfish reasons?

Chapter 8

~

The Nightshade Universe

Afton was searching for Beryth when she was summoned to her father's common hall. The warriors had returned from the Troyk penal colony. Her heart beat a little faster knowing Lorenz had returned. Quickening her step, Afton practically ran to comply with Yorik's request.

When she reached her destination, the hall was in chaos. The vampires were attempting to divide up the rewards from battle, namely the warriors from the losing side. The prisoners were not complying with what her father's guards were trying to do.

The initial shock that vampires existed had worn off. At this point, the men figured they had nothing to lose in being defiant, they were dead either way. They did not realize there was a vicious quick death and a long, lingering one as a blood donor. Afton was not sure which was worse.

It did not take long to spot Lorenz in the melee of vampires and captives before her. He was calmly talking to Drake, as if havoc was an everyday affair. When he spotted her, Lorenz said something to Drake and then made his way to her side. He had taken off the neck guard, but still wore his breast plate. He looked so handsome and rugged, heat was rushing through her body in response. In this getup, he looked more like a medieval warlord, than a vampire. His face was rosy from the amount of blood he must have consumed during the battle.

"Welcome back," Afton said. She barely got the words out, her throat was so dry. It was a rather lame comment, but she was barely holding it together being once again in his presence. The disarray she had been watching melted to the background as he stood before her. He was the only reality now in her universe.

"I have arranged for Ginkgo Terra animal blood to be provided for you," Lorenz whispered in her ear. He smelled of smoke and death, but she pushed those thoughts away. "Unfortunately, there is no getting around you participating in the victory ceremony, which is about to take place. As Yorik's daughter, you must drink from the fallen. It is more symbolic than taking blood for nourishment. Take as much or as little as you desire, but do not attempt to deceive your father in pretending to partake."

A trumpet sounded. Afton assumed it was the beginning of the ritual Lorenz had warned her about. Her father had made it quite clear what his expectations were. As if they were about to begin a play, everyone took their places. Lorenz guided her to stand next to Yorik. He did not remove the hand he had on her shoulder. She felt more confident with Lorenz's flesh on her bare skin. Heat generated from the spot and spread throughout her body. She could feel sweat running down the small of her back.

"Let the defeated be brought forward," Yorik announced in a loud, booming voice. Afton watched as several of the struggling men were brought before them and chained to the floor. "My daughter and I will take our fill from these pathetic warriors before those that fought so valiantly are justly rewarded."

Lorenz guided her, as Afton walked alongside her father. The whole ceremony disgusted her, she was relieved Lorenz was there to support her. Afton doubted she would have been able to do this without him. She was not sure what these men had done, but for her own sanity, she assumed the worst.

Removing a knife from his boot, Lorenz grabbed one of the prisoner's arms and slashed his wrist. There was a viciousness in the action she had never seen from Lorenz before. Blood quickly ran from the cut as Lorenz lifted the extremity for Afton's use.

She placed her mouth around the wound and drank in the life affirming liquid. As with all the human blood she had drunk since arriving here, it was delicious. Originally she was only going to take a token amount, but it tasted so good. Afton was lost in her own blood lust. For the first time, she used her teeth to deepen the cut. These men were murderers and rapists, she was not drinking from an innocent. She had somehow been able to see the sins the man had been guilty of. His cries fell on deaf ears as Afton drank.

When she realized what she had done, she attempted to back away. Lorenz held her in place, applying very little pressure. Afton could have easily broken his hold on her. It was his way of communicating she had done nothing wrong in feeding as she had. Maybe it was time to realize she was not human, but a hybrid. Her declining health could be a result of her backing off before her body was able to get the volume of blood she truly needed.

She bit a little harder. Adrenaline now pumping into the blood and its addition made all the difference in the world. Fear laced in the blood was feeding her cells like nothing she had experienced before. The human side of her won out, as she backed away from her victim in horror.

Lorenz lifted her in his arms and carried her out before her father realized what had happened. She could feel his anger rippling off him in waves. Had he merely pretended to be kind to her to get her trust? A feeling of doom consumed what little brain capacity she had left.

The girl had so little self-preservation, it angered Lorenz. If her father had sensed her backing off from her symbolic reward, Lorenz did not know if he would have been able to protect her from Yorik's fury. Lorenz's ancient blood provided him greater strength against any vampire, with the exception of a frenzied master vampire. Afton started to feed properly from the human when she recoiled from the experience.

When he reached Afton's rooms, his guards opened the door and maintained their posts outside. He placed the girl on her feet, still too angry to say anything. Words said in anger were hard to retract.

"What did I do wrong?" the girl cried, tears running down her cheeks. Lorenz had not realized she had started to cry. He had always been able to disregard the tears his victims shed, but these were different. Shame consumed him for not taking into account everything Afton had gone through.

He took her into his arms. "You must never back-off from feeding. It is a sign of weakness."

Afton shoved him away. If he had cared to keep her where she currently was, it would have taken little effort to continue to hold her. Obviously, the girl needed space. He could at least give her that for the time being. It was getting harder not to dominate Afton as his body and soul wanted.

"You stink of smoke and spoiled blood," Afton said in anger. She paced in front of him. Venting her anger, she was working to get it under control. "Why must I be as brutal as my father?"

"It is time you stop looking through your human eyes," Lorenz replied, matching anger with anger. "Although I am stating the obvious, we are vampires, Afton. We are a brutal, unmerciful race. How else do you think we have been able to survive longer than the humans on your former planet have been standing erect?"

Now it was Lorenz, who needed to pace and release his frustration. How was he going to break through her timid interior and bring out the vampire half of her that should have a survival instinct? She had been human too long. If she did not change mentally, she would not survive long in his world, regardless of what he did to protect her.

They continued to pace, throwing aggravated looks back and forth. He could handle going to war and tearing his enemies apart, but dealing with this little girl was proving to be harder than he had anticipated.

"There is a shower through that door," Afton indicated to her left. "I cannot take the stench of you any longer."

Getting naked in such close proximity to Afton was probably not a good idea. However, he did not want to leave her alone. He was not sure what the aftermath of the vampire warrior ritual would bring. If any members of The League had participated in the ceremony, they would be after Afton's blood this very night. Although he had four guards outside her door, he did not want to leave her.

"You are welcome to join me," Lorenz said in a playful manner. Maybe changing his strategy would warm her up a bit. He did not want to be her adversary. Her rightful place was in his arms.

"Dream on, Romeo," Afton muttered under her breath. He could not miss her pupils dilating at the invitation.

Laughing to himself, Lorenz made his way to the washroom. He purposely left the door ajar, as he started to undress. Unfortunately, the clothing he discarded would have to be burned. They were saturated with blood and terribly discolored by smoke. Naked, he entered the shower stall and turned on the water, setting it to the highest heat setting. His body could withstand any temperature, however he liked the steam, which accompanied near scalding water. If Afton chose to join him, he would willingly reduce the heat.

The water pounding against his back felt wonderful. As expected, the glass enclosure was now fogged from the volume of steam generated. He pushed the compulsion for Afton to join him. They had not shared blood, but he had nothing to lose in trying to tempt her to shower with him.

To his surprise, the shower door opened and Afton stood there still dressed. "I want to see you," she said. The gust of steam hit her limp black hair, causing it to curl. He could once again see the radiant creature he saw when he first laid eyes on her. He adjusted the water temperature as she walked into the shower, fully clothed.

Afton placed her hands on his chest and started to trace along the contours of his muscles. Unconsciously, she pushed back wisps of wet hair that journeyed to her face. Lorenz was hesitant to take her into his arms at this point. He gave her the freedom to take this as far as she felt comfortable. As she continued to explore his upper body, his rod was getting harder than he ever thought possible. This had turned out to be a terrible idea.

Afton never touched a man as she was touching Lorenz. She thought he would be cold to the touch, but the exact opposite was true. As she moved her palm up and down his chest, her hand was warmed by his body. The hot water acted as a means to cool down the heat generated from the skin on skin contact.

She felt Lorenz holding back. It was something she sensed, rather than anything he did outwardly. So much of what she felt for the vampire before her were feelings and impressions. None of it made any sense to her. Her world had been turned upside down. Since arriving in the Nightshade universe she has spent most of her time reacting.

The rare occasions she put thought into her actions, the end results were disastrous. This was one of the few enjoyable moments she had experienced since leaving Earth. She was going to enjoy it for as long as she could.

Daring to get closer, Afton stepped forward. Lorenz immediately folded her into his arms and brought his lips down to meet hers. The kiss started tentatively, a mere brush, more apt for strangers to exchange. Afton moved further into his arms, wanting more of what Lorenz had to offer. His lips grew more aggressive as he applied more pressure and forced her lips open with his tongue. To be truthful, Afton did not put up much of a defense.

As the juices of their mouths blended, Afton felt the adrenaline surge through her body. The sensation was not unlike earlier today when she had deepened the cut with her teeth from the man she drank from. This time she did not back away from the sensation. She welcomed it.

The euphoria she was experiencing ended abruptly when Lorenz grabbed the bottom of her dress and started to lift it. She grabbed his hands and brought her dress back down below her knees. Being inexperienced, she had not expected this type of response from him.

"I want to see you," Lorenz growled. It appeared the primal beast within him was angered by Afton's action. "We are to join together, as mates are destined to do."

Afton was ashamed of her declining body. The thought of Lorenz looking at her naked and finding her lacking was more than she could handle. Somehow she needed to find a way to gain weight and fill out. She had always been slight and sickly, but she wanted to be so much more for Lorenz.

"Not now," she pleaded with Lorenz. "Maybe if I am more aggressive in my eating habits, I will be able to put some flesh on my bones. I don't want you to feel bone when you touch me, but soft, supple flesh."

Afton had wanted to hide the misery she was feeling when she addressed Lorenz. The look on his face told her she had failed. She saw pity in his lovely blue eyes. It was the last thing she wanted from this man.

"Drink from me and become strong," Lorenz said. "Through the joining, you will be everything you have ever desired."

How Afton wished those words were true. She was still mortified by her violent reaction to Drake's blood and Lorenz assisting her when she became ill. The thought of getting sick after she drank Lorenz's blood was more than she could bear. This was not how she imagined their first sexual encounter going. Without meaning to, a little cry escaped from her mouth.

Horrified, she revealed too much, she exited the shower. Her dress hung to her like a second skin. At least the material added substance to her body where in reality, there was very little.

Lorenz was right behind her. She turned around as he grabbed a towel and wrapped it around his waist. Yet again, she was overwhelmed by his beauty. Feelings of inadequacy depleted whatever self-confidence she had left. Afton felt absolutely wretched. She wanted to crawl into the closest hole and disappear.

"We are going to have to join eventually," Lorenz announced. "The sooner we get it over with, the better."

"I am not some foul medicine you have to choke down," Afton cried. She was mortified her voice cracked as she finished her sentence. His words further diminished her feelings of self-worth. She was stupid to believe the beautiful, powerful creature she stood before would want her.

"That did not come out as I intended," Lorenz apologized. He reached for a robe and handed it to her. "You should get out of those wet clothes before you catch a chill. Remove that wet rag and join me in the other room so we can continue this discussion."

Afton stood there as Lorenz gave her the privacy she needed to undress. It was not lost on her that she would have nothing on under the robe and he was only wearing a towel.

Her body started to heat as she remembered how he looked in the shower. If only she could turn off her brain and let her body have its due. She understood what Lorenz was referring to when he said they needed to get on with the joining. Afton was the barrier. Once she let go of her inhibitions, they both would be in a better place. Perhaps they would then be able to leave this terrible place and journey to Lorenz's home.

Shedding the wet fabric from her body, she threw the sopping mess in the corner. The plush robe she wrapped around her still damp body felt wonderful. She imagined Lorenz's arms once again around her. It was time to face the music and rejoin him. She envisioned entering her bedroom several times before she gathered the nerve to do so in reality.

Rather than still being draped in a towel, Lorenz was once again in slacks and a shirt. Without warning, Lorenz charged toward her and tackled her onto the bed. He pulled back her robe and took her breast into his mouth. His tongue swirled around her nipple, as Afton placed her hands in his lovely wavy blond hair. Thrilled Lorenz took the initiative for them to make love, Afton pulled him closer to her body.

A pounding on the door broke the spell they had both been under. Lorenz muttered under his breath, as he rose to see who was demanding their attention. Afton quickly covered herself and better secured the robe.

"Yorik has demanded your company," a vampire she had seen on many occasions informed them. "The girl can remain here. Drake has mentioned the possibility of opening relations with the Troyk universe. Our master wishes to get your opinion on what you witnessed during the battle."

Afton could feel the vampire's eyes exploring her unkempt appearance. Self-consciously she wrapped her arms around her chest. It was the first time she had been looked at by another vampire in that fashion. The warmth she had felt earlier, was now replaced with feelings of revulsion.

"I have to go," Lorenz told her. "I will return as soon as I am able."

"The discussions will probably take some time," the vampire stated. "Is there anything I can do to assist you while Lorenz is otherwise occupied?"

A chill ran down Afton's spine. Although he probably was just being polite, Afton was bothered by this vampire's attention. Lorenz picked up the same menacing vibe, as he placed a hand on her shoulder. He gently squeezed her, communicating his understanding of her physical concerns.

"The girl is fine," Lorenz answered for her. "You may accompany me back to Yorik. My guards will continue to protect and cater to my intended's needs."

Lorenz left with the vampire, saying nothing to Afton. She could still feel the warmth, where his hand had been on her shoulder. Afton would not rest easy until Lorenz was back in her company. An uneasiness created by the vampire who had entered her room was not easily remedied.

Malice carried the towels into the girl's room. He needed to start referring to himself by another name as he continued to plan the girl's demise. It made it more exciting, a departure from his dreary day to day life. After he was done with Afton and her blood fortified his decaying body, perhaps he would start a hive of his own. His notoriety would draw others like him to his own stronghold. He had a property not far from here that would offer a respectable start.

He walked past Lorenz's guards with no issues. The fools did not realize the threat he represented. Unfortunately, he did not want to merely kill her, it would be too easy. He was within range to bring her down before the guards were able to react. No, he wanted to possess her first.

She smiled at him as he laid the towels on the cabinet just inside her bathroom. He looked at the shower and imagined her naked underneath the water. Perhaps he would allow her the ability to wash the blood from her body after some of their sessions together. His member grew hard as he continued to fantasize all he would do.

She had been magnificent during the ritual. He almost came in his pants when the girl tore the flesh of the prisoner she was feeding from. The loss of control she exhibited let him know they would have years of fun together. Afton had the makings of becoming as great a monster as he was. Malice would mold her into what he most wanted in a partner, a woman to spend eternity with. Perhaps he would not kill her after all.

The foolish girl thanked him as he turned to leave. A small smile radiated from her face that caused him a moment's hesitation. A foreign feeling of warmth started to spread through his body, like an unchecked cancer. It must be some type of witchcraft she wielded that made him have such unnatural feelings. He would beat her until she would be incapable of casting any spells on him again.

He just needed to be patient. His time would come.

Chapter 9

Afton woke early, anxious to see Lorenz. Amazed at her uncharacteristic behavior of entering the shower the previous night, she wanted to further explore her body's reaction to his presence. She felt great, by some miracle she slept through the night. It was the first time some nightmare had not woken her in a shivering, cold sweat.

Her life had become a nightmare, why wouldn't her dreams reflect the horror she lived? Although she did not remember her dreams from the night before, she knew they were filled with lovely episodes with her future husband. She dared to hope her life was about to change for the better.

Eager to see Lorenz, she quickly showered and dressed. For the first time since arriving in the Nightshade universe, she was actually looking forward to her day. Depression quickly replaced her elated mood. All it took was looking in the mirror and seeing the near skeleton before her. Under closer examination, she noticed her lips were still somewhat swollen from last night's incredible kisses. Warmth coursed through her body as she remembered what he had done to her.

A knock on the door shook her from her thoughts. Lorenz entered, looking incredible as ever. Today he wore a rich burgundy shirt and black slacks that hugged his incredible muscular thighs. Relieved he dressed differently from the other vampires, her eyes continued to appreciate the man before her. Her fingers became restless, wanting to touch his chest, as they did the night before. She balled her hands into a fist, not wanting to be obvious where her thoughts drove her.

He came up to her and grabbed her fisted hand, bringing it to his lips for a kiss. Her hand relaxed and opened like a flower greets the morning sun. A force within her wanted to emerge, but did not know how. It was the oddest feeling, almost as if she was developing another personality. Perhaps a defense mechanism from within was finally germinating to help her cope with everything she had endured.

"Your father has requested our presence," Lorenz informed her. He was so formal in his words, appearance, and movement. She had the urge to mess up his perfectly coiffed hair.

"Requested seems a bit passive of a word to use where my father is concerned," Afton said. She wanted to lighten the discussion between them. Everything around her was dark and foreboding, her time with this man was her one escape.

"None the less," Lorenz continued, "it is not wise to keep Yorik waiting."

Afton knew firsthand how volatile her father could be, she had the bruises to prove it. Submitting to the request seemed judicious. At this point in time, she was not sure if Lorenz had the strength to take on her father and win. Although he had royal blood, she was not sure if it was a matter of respect or physical power the ancient blood commanded. She had been told Drake and Lorenz had been created by the original vampire, but she did not understand what that meant. It was difficult gathering information from her servants, she had to be satisfied with what little she had been able to garner.

They walked the deserted hallways in silence. After last night, she was not sure where their relationship was heading. Like anything new, it was fragile. Fearing the wrong words would create a setback, Afton followed Lorenz's lead by keeping her mouth shut.

Their footsteps along the stone walkway serenaded them as they moved forward. She played with the pace of her steps to change the tempo playing in her head. Happy for any distraction from the dismal requirement to see her father and the silence presented by Lorenz.

When they reached her father's public chamber Afton was surprised to find him alone. Having delivered their charges to their destination, the guards who had accompanied them left their side. They would remain outside the chamber until Afton was ready to return to her rooms. With her curiosity piqued, Afton approached her father with Lorenz beside her.

"Why is it my daughter still looks like the walking dead?" Yorik inquired, sarcasm dripping from the words he uttered. Her father had not once complimented anything Afton had done or her appearance, so his words did not have the impact she was certain he meant to inflict. At this point, anything he said went in one ear and out the other.

"She reacted violently to the blood Drake volunteered." Lorenz was quick to answer her father's question. "I did not want to risk Afton losing what little strength she still possesses. I have arranged for the animal blood, she drank and thrived on while she lived on Earth, to be delivered."

Afton involuntarily stepped back, remembering the rage Yorik exhibited after she had previously asked for animal blood. Almost immediately, Lorenz's arm coiled around her back and pulled her back to his side. It horrified her he had noted her reaction to his statement. Her behavior certainly did not give Lorenz the impression she believed he could not protect Afton from her father. She straightened, as if a rod had been placed along her spine.

"Perhaps I overreacted when Afton made the request originally," Yorik admitted. "If you have been able to secure the assistance of the crystal telepath you mentioned last night, I suppose that will suffice for the short-term.

"Only by you joining with my daughter, will she truly be able to transform. Prudence dictates I will not allow her to leave the confines of this stronghold until that transformation has been initiated. The League has hunted her for as long as she has lived. You are the only hope she has going forward."

"The League?" Afton inquired. Obviously, her father and Lorenz were more aware of the dangers that surrounded her than she did. It was only fair she be told what plots were present and why her father all of a sudden seemed like one of the good guys. Ignorance never did anyone any good.

"There is an organization that believes in the purity of the vampire race," her father explained. "Their one mission is to destroy women who can reproduce with our kind and eliminate any offspring from those unions. When Lorenz rescued your mother from their clutches, I knew he was strong enough to guarantee your future."

"That is why you entered the treaty with me?" Surprise evident in Lorenz's voice.

"How else would I get you to enter a joining with a half-ling?" Yorik responded. "You had been a member of that group since its inception."

Afton gasped at that revelation. The man that stood before her had killed the very thing she was. Afton was between two monsters and it appeared her father was the better of the two.

⤜⟡

To say Lorenz was dreading the moment Afton learned of his past affiliation with The League was an understatement. Now looking at the betrayal reflected in her lovely eyes, he had underestimated how horrible he would feel. Then again, he had not expected to care for the girl as deeply as he did now. Last night's kiss just confirmed how badly he wanted Afton. It tore at his heart watching her gravitate to her father's side.

Lorenz stood in silence as he searched for the words to explain why he joined the group. Everything that came to mind would only dig him into a deeper hole. He saw the desperation in her expression, as he continued to be mute on the subject.

"Vampires are not meant to breed," her father finally explained. "There are those among us who believe that it is a miracle when life is created out of what is meant to be a sterile race. Unfortunately, The League looks at the weak children born from such unions and believes both the child and the mother are unnatural. It is not unlike the racial cleansing factions within your old world, Afton."

Unfamiliar with what Yorik spoke of, Lorenz knew he did not do him any favors by the look of disgust on Afton's face. She rubbed her hands up and down her arm, as if she was trying to brush off the remnants of his touch. He knew he could no longer stand there in silence.

"I cannot excuse what I did in the past, Afton," Lorenz pleaded. "Somehow the words I heard for so long about how vampires were created, not born, made sense. If I had it to do all over again, I would have made better choices.

"The fact Drake deplored the group should have broken through my thick skull sooner than it did. For several millennia, I attended meetings, not truly understanding the horror I was supporting. When it dawned on me what they were really doing, I left the group and saved as many lives as I could."

"One of those lives was your mother's," Yorik added. "I mistreated her terribly. When I finally had the ability to reproduce, I was not going to let your mother's feelings stand in my way."

"Yes, you are certainly father of the year." Obviously Afton had not planned to say those words out loud. Lorenz watched as she covered her mouth with her hands, horrified she had verbalized her thoughts.

Fortunately, Yorik did not seem disturbed by her words. Yorik knew he was a monster; he did not pretend to be something he was not. Lorenz wished he could say the same. He had provided intelligence that led to the demise of several women. Ashamed of what he did, Lorenz knew he would spend the rest of his life atoning for his actions.

"When I learned The League had captured your pregnant mother, I knew I had to get personally involved." Lorenz needed to plead his case. "One of my associates worked with a crystal telepath. I was able to barter for his assistance. He aided me in saving your mother and ultimately rescued her from this universe."

"Markus," Afton said, more to herself, rather than addressing him and Yorik. "My mother never recovered from his death. She took her life shortly after he died from a brain hemorrhage. After everything she had been through, my mother could not live without him. Theirs was a true tragic love story." Tears fell from her eyes as she mourned her mother and the crystal telepath who had saved both their lives.

"Your only hope for survival, Afton, is to join with Lorenz," Yorik said.

His words pulled Afton out of whatever melancholy mood she had fallen into remembering her mother. Afton looked at her father, shaking her head. It was not a giant leap to know what he said was not well received by his daughter. She barely looked in Lorenz's direction and when she did, Afton could not look him in the eye. He was relieved at this point, Lorenz knew he would not like what he would see reflected in them.

"What exactly is involved in joining?" Afton asked in a timid voice. Self-preservation had taken over her train of thought. Lorenz imagined she was not going to like what her father was about to share. A part of him figured she already knew the answer to her question and only asked to validate her assumptions.

"There is first a blood exchange," Yorik answered. "The strength of the bonding will determine what happens after the mingling of each other's blood in your systems. It is best to take it from the carotid artery. The flow is strong and the blood is rich. The changes vary from merely enriching your body's cells, to the ability to communicate telepathically."

"And secondly?"

"Intercourse," Afton's father replied. So much for being delicate and working slowly to what must be shared. After last night, Lorenz wished he could tell her they would make love. He had never experienced the emotions which consumed him during their interlude in the shower. After everything she had just learned about him, he imagined those words would not ring true.

Afton's reaction was as strong as he expected. "No!" she shouted and stormed from the hall.

Lorenz knew he had to go after her and explain what could be gained after they made love. He saw the evidence every time he looked at her. There was not a doubt in Lorenz's mind that she would transform. That beautiful, healthy vision he saw would one day be Afton's reality. However, that woman would never see the light of day if Afton could not tolerate being in the same room with him.

There was no way in hell she was going to have sex with that monster. He had a lovely exterior, but inside he was deplorable. Under different circumstances, Lorenz would have quietly stood by while she was murdered by one of his League brethren. Numerous men followed her, but she knew the vampire she wanted to see the least was among them. Lorenz had crept into her heart and betrayed her trust. He was not what he presented himself to be.

When she got to her rooms, she slammed the door behind her. Unfortunately, it had no lock. There was no way to keep him from her presence. Most of her guards were provided by Lorenz and they would not protect her from him. It was not a surprise when he entered her room almost immediately after her arrival.

"We have to talk," Lorenz said, with a determination in his voice she had not heard before.

Afton knew she could ignore him, but that would not get rid of him or make her feel any better. "Get out," she screamed. He had hurt her more than she ever imagined possible. It was impossible to speak without her voice shaking with the betrayal she suffered.

"I am not the man I was when I joined that group thousands of years ago."

What a hypocrite! "For thousands of years you were a member of a group that killed women and children. You really expect me to believe that one day you woke up and had a revelation that what you believed in was wrong and all of a sudden you were a new vampire?"

For a time she had no longer thought of him as a monster, but as a man, but that had changed. He might dress differently and not possess the blood lusting eyes, but he was as much a reprehensible beast as those animals that surrounded her father.

"Actions speak louder than words, Afton. I rescued your mother before The League could torture and force her to miscarry you. In all those centuries I belonged to The League, I never physically harmed the women they went after or the children they destroyed. Maybe if I had, I would have left the group much earlier. There is a reason why I had kept my allegiance to that group a secret from Drake. Deep down inside I knew they were wrong."

"Am I supposed to give you a medal?"

Afton did something she never imagined she could do. She went up to Lorenz and slapped him across the face with all her might. He barely moved from the impact, while her palm stung, but she felt a little better. She was expecting some type of retaliation, but what Lorenz did next surprised her.

Within an instant of her slap, Lorenz took Afton into his arms and kissed her. It was not a gentle kiss, like the ones they had shared last night. This kiss was laced with anger and passion. Had he not had his hands acting as vises around her upper arms, she would have fallen to her knees. Her treacherous body reacted to his kiss, as her brain went dormant.

When he deepened the kiss, she clutched onto him, as if she would fall into an endless void and he was required to ground her. If he held her any tighter, her bones would break. Groaning would only encourage him.

She patted him twice on the arm, hoping the universal sign of drowning would be recognizable by someone who lived in another dimension. He must have recognized her distress, as he lightened his hold on her. She wrapped her arms around his neck and continued to savor his kiss. Everything she had learned about his past seemed to evaporate with his touch.

Lorenz bit the side of his cheek and blood trickled into her mouth. Yorik's words about the blood exchange came flowing into her brain. Panic ensued, as she struggled to break the kiss and liberate herself from his embrace. He did not present any resistance to Afton's desire to escape.

"What have you done?" Afton cried. She ran into the bathroom and spit out the blood still present.

"Only what was necessary." Lorenz was so glib in his delivery, she wanted to slap him again. Her condition had always limited what she could do, but Afton had the freedom to make what decisions she could. Between her father and Lorenz, she felt every aspect of her life was being manipulated.

"You have no right," she cried.

"In that you are wrong," Lorenz responded. He entered the bathroom and grabbed her arm. "You belong to me by contract. I refuse to see you wasting away when there is something I can do about it. Whatever I have to do to ensure you are healthy, I will not hesitate to do. Tomorrow we will do the blood exchange, whether you are agreeable or not. This ridiculous game is over. The other fluid exchange will take place when we are under the protection of my home."

The coward masked his true intent in ambiguous terms. Afton knew exactly what he had planned. Fate was having her walk in her mother's footsteps. Unable to hold them back any longer, sobs escaped from her tormented soul.

Lorenz released her and stormed out of her rooms without turning around or addressing her again. She staggered out of the bathroom and lay on her perfectly made bed. How was she going to stop Lorenz from taking her blood and forcing her to drink his? What would happen to her once they performed the joining?

Chapter 10

~

Barely having recovered from her last interchange with Lorenz, Afton was unprepared when he entered her room. She shifted on the bed, bracing her back against the headboard. In the little time she had to think about the blood exchange, Afton decided it was futile to fight.

There was always the possibility she would enjoy the joining. Her body had reacted to his touch, sometimes in opposition to what her brain thought. Besides, she would not last much longer with her body wasting away daily. Her defensive move upon his unexpected appearance did not surprise her, she was still struggling with what she had decided to accept as her fate. Although she knew he would not turn her over to The League, his past association with them still bothered her.

"The female crystal telepath has returned," Lorenz stated. "Drake has requested we join him."

Afton shot out of bed, consumed with concern for Alex. She hoped the little redhead had not accompanied her friend back into the Nightshade universe. The welfare of that baby was Afton's primary concern. As she took her first step, a wave of nausea washed over her. Her condition continued to deteriorate. Like it or not, she needed to initiate the joining with Lorenz. If she was going to save the unborn child, Afton needed the strength only the sharing of blood promised.

"Feed me your blood," Afton commanded. Lorenz hesitated, obviously surprised by her change of heart. She needed to reassure him she was not doing this under duress. "Only a few sips to prepare my body for the true joining."

Perhaps she would be able to digest a small amount of his blood. What little she may have digested before did not seem to have done any harm.

Lorenz bit his wrist and brought it to her lips. "It is from a vein, hopefully it will not have the potency to make you ill."

The crimson gold exploded in her mouth. Energy surged through her body, feeding her starving cells. Drake's blood seemed anemic compared to Lorenz's. It took all her willpower to release his wrist from her mouth. Time was limited, she now needed Lorenz to drink from her. In the weeks she had been in the Nightshade world, no vampire had attempted to take her blood. Afton timidly extended her arm, an invitation she knew Lorenz would be unable to resist.

He took her arm and pulled her closer. With the precision of Don Juan, Lorenz peeled off the top of her dress. The material hugged her hips, as Lorenz removed her bra. It was the first time she was exposed to any man. She was so captivated by what he was doing, Afton did not worry about his reaction to her pathetic body.

Lorenz laid her on the bed and took one of her breasts into his mouth. Afton sucked in her breath, as sensations ran through her body. He released her breast, only to cup it in his hand. Lifting his head, Lorenz made eye contact with her. A grin crossed his face before he once again brought his mouth down on her.

For the first time, she saw his incisors elongate, ready to take her blood. She closed her eyes and leaned her head back against the pillows. His teeth brushed the outer mound, until a slight pinprick shot through her flesh. Pleasure the likes of which she never dreamed possible consumed her. Lorenz had barely sucked in her blood before he released her. Although she knew Drake was waiting, she felt a sense of loss when Lorenz released her breast.

It had been a small blood exchange, probably not enough to constitute a joining. Afton felt no different, but had not experienced another spell of dizziness when Lorenz brought her to her feet. She also seemed to have digested the blood she had taken from him with ease.

"That was just a taste of what we will share together," Lorenz said as he redressed her. "I had always heard that half-ling blood was ambrosia, but I never realized the power of it. It has to be you, Afton. Otherwise, vampires would never have destroyed other half-lings. You are unique, at least where we are concerned. For the first time in my long existence, I am beginning to believe the tales about vampire soul mates."

Afton was so overwhelmed by his words and what happened, she barely had the presence of mind to assist him. What had not been lost on her was Lorenz brushing his tongue against the small incision he had created in order to take her blood. For the first time she had witnessed a vampire healing his willing victim. But she had not been a victim, and she wanted more.

Afton was in such a dazed state, she barely was aware of them arriving in her father's great hall. A woman's gasp brought her back to the world around her. Fortunately, Alex was not among the visitors. Shirl and Starc were present, as well as a tall brown haired woman and a man chained to the floor.

"My daughter's appearance shocks you, warrior?" her father said in a conversational voice. He obviously was addressing the tall Amazon who gasped when Afton entered the room. Every morning when she looked in the mirror, she knew what an awful sight she presented. "The solution to her health is right in front of her, but she refuses to succumb to what is in her best interest."

The minimal blood exchanged she enjoyed with Lorenz flooded her mind as Shirl tried to convince her father Afton should leave with them for her own well-being. Previous discussions on the topic had been painful for Afton, since she knew there was no escaping her father's world. Now, she had no desire to leave. It was still embarrassing to be the topic of conversation. As before, Afton chose to say nothing.

Her eyes wandered to the man chained to the floor. He had attacked Alex and endangered her unborn child. Alex's friends had brought her attacker to the Nightshade universe to punish him. Drake had taken ownership of the pathetic creature.

Afton had never seen Drake so angry, so close to losing control. His actions were a direct reflection of what he felt for the unborn child. Before the crystal telepath left with her friends, Drake promised the man's punishment would be severe enough to offset the degree of his crime. For once, Afton did not feel pity for one of the vampire's victims.

She felt a sense of loss after Shirl and the others left. Other than her time with Lorenz, she was isolated in this world. So absorbed in her own misery, Afton did not notice her father approach, until he had a hold of her chin.

"It has started." Yorik seemed pleased. "I do not understand why you have not completed the joining, but I am pleased you have finally been claimed, my daughter." Her father released her and turned toward Lorenz. "My spies have picked up coded messages from The League. It is time you both leave this place and venture to your own stronghold."

Drake moved toward the prisoner and released him from the chains. "I will be leaving with Lorenz and Afton. It is my intention to take this blood sack with me."

"He is yours," her father replied. "Remain with them until the transformation is complete. I know he is your blood brother. I will continue to overlook all the injuries you have inflicted upon me, if you will safeguard my daughter until the danger has passed."

With those words, her father left the chamber. Afton felt a loss of a relationship she never had with Yorik. It would have been out of character for him to have embraced her, but how she had longed for it. Rather than showing physical signs of caring, her father had safeguarded her future. A future solely dependent on the vampire who stood beside her.

Lorenz watched Yorik exit the chamber after he had been told to leave with Afton. The girl stood meekly by his side. How different she was when he drank from her breast. He could feel the excitement coursing through her, which only fueled his desire to complete the joining. Once she has transformed, Afton would be his equal.

There had been so little blood interchanged, no physical changes were evident as yet. She had at least been able to tolerate the blood she had taken from him. Her system had not rejected it, as it had Drake's. He was actually thankful she was unable to digest his blood brother's blood, Afton was his.

"Plan to leave within the next hour," Lorenz advised Drake. "The crystal telepath who promised to deliver blood from Ginkgo Terra should be here shortly." He turned and looked at the pale creature next to him. "There is nothing here worth taking with us. Personally, I would like to burn all the white dresses you have been forced to wear. The male crystal telepath promised to bring clothes you will feel comfortable in, when he returns from Earth."

As if entering on cue, the portal opened once again. The tall Troyk crystal telepath with the sun-bleached hair exited the portal. A second man was with him, who Lorenz had met in the penal colony world. Both men carried several bags.

"I see Shirl beat us here," Darden said, looking down at the man chained to the floor. "We can finally have some peace, no longer having to worry about Raine Narmouth."

For the first time since entering the hall Afton found her voice. "Are Alex and the baby all right?" Lorenz was pleased she was concerned with the well-being of another. It must reduce the anxiety she must have felt about her own situation.

"They are fine. We waited until the med-tech was done with the exam before we left," Koel replied. This was the man who had planned the rescue of his friends from the penal colony. Although Lorenz had limited contact with the man, he respected his tactical skills. If possible, he needed to find a way to stay in contact with him, in case he needed help in planning any actions he needed to take against The League.

"The one named Shirl," Lorenz said, "she can open a portal anywhere, is that not correct?"

Darden and Koel shared a look between the two of them. Drake had shared how his crystal telepath had escaped from their world earlier. Yorik had also commented several times on the extreme power a mated female crystal telepath possessed.

"It is not my intention to put her in any danger," Lorenz shared with them. "We have a faction in this world which tries to eliminate half-lings, like Afton. At this point we have been able to protect her within her father's keep. Drake, Afton, and I will be leaving for my own stronghold. I may wish to leverage Koel's skills to help safeguard her, as well as provide you with the location for future blood deliveries. My home does not contain a natural portal."

"Shirl has the blood opal Drake gave her," Koel replied. "Within the week we will travel back and request safe-passage to your home. At that point, Shirl will be able to open a portal within your home and determine the frequency to return directly there when required. I have my own trip to make to claim my soul mate from the Gingko Terra world."

"Thank you," Afton once again spoke. She had taken one of the bottles of blood that had been delivered and quickly drank. "God, that is awful. I have been forced to drink human blood here. This stuff is foul compared to what I have become accustomed to."

"Whatever they inject the livestock with sustained you better than most of the blood you consumed here." Lorenz did not feel it necessary to mention that his own blood would transform the near specter before them. Once she went through the conversion, he hoped she would no longer have to drink the animal blood from Ginkgo Terra.

Darden approached Afton, cautiously, keeping one eye on Lorenz. "I am not happy about what we were forced to do to get Shirl back from this world. Shirl particularly feels guilty about our kidnapping you from your world. We even stooped to using mind control to get you to enter the portal.

"Ben and Cassie Clark, as they presented themselves to you, have the ability to use mind control telepathy. Cassie got you out of your dorm room and Benko convinced you to see your father. We knew the type of world we were condemning you to." Darden took Afton into his arms. "I am so sorry. Anytime you are ready to go home, we will take you there."

Lorenz had to hold himself back from killing the man as he held Afton. He knew it was an embrace between friends, as well as the man's way of apologizing for his role in what had happened to her. Yet, he could not help but to feel jealous with Afton in another man's arms.

Before Lorenz was able to react to Darden's invitation to return her to Earth, Afton replied to Darden. "I do not know what Lorenz's home will be like, but for the first time in my life, I have hope that I may actually find a place I can live in peace. Tell Shirl not to beat herself up on my account. She should direct her energies to safeguarding the child Alex is carrying."

Smart girl, Lorenz thought. She gave Darden enough warning without mentioning the threat Drake could present to the chameleon's daughter. Lorenz was grateful for having Afton, he could not deny his friend the same happiness. But what price would that child have to pay?

"You should go, and we need to prepare to travel to my home," Lorenz directed those around him.

"I will take care of this one." Drake pointed to Raine Narmouth who still cowered on the floor.

The Troyk men left through the portal that could have easily taken Afton to Ginkgo Terra. Was he being selfish holding on to the girl? He could have freed himself from having to safeguard Afton and Yorik would have not known. Somehow he knew it would be the biggest mistake he ever made if he let her slip through his fingers.

An uneasiness came upon him regarding the trip he was about to take to his stronghold. The trip back to his home should present little danger, yet something nagged at him. He knew he would not be able to relax until they were safely behind the stone walls of his own keep.

Chapter 11

~

Afton felt like she was traveling in a large coffin. The train carriage contained no windows and traveled approximately six feet under the surface. The significance of the subterranean distance was not lost on her. The train was designed to protect the vampires who traveled from settlement to settlement from the harmful rays of the sun. A vampire, regardless of age, could not tolerate any exposure to the sun. Burying the tracks farther safeguarded the occupants in case of the rare derailment. Although the car was comfortable enough, Afton could not help but be a little claustrophobic. The use of satin material, just like in coffins, also freaked her out a bit.

Throughout the journey Lorenz and Drake talked about vampire politics. It was a subject she should have been interested in considering this was her new home. However, the conversation bored her to tears and there was no scenery to enjoy as they made their way to Lorenz's stronghold. Having only stayed in her father's keep, Afton had no idea what the surface of Nightshade looked like. Were there trees and flowers that graced this parallel world? Perhaps when they arrived at Lorenz's, Afton would be able to take walks outside the settlement.

A scary thought crossed her mind as she dreamed of walking in this world. What would happen if the blood exchange made her super sensitive to sunlight, preventing her from ever enjoying a sunny day again? One of her dark moods came upon her, the first she had since arriving. Up to this point she was strictly in survival mode, experiencing a constant level of anxiety during each waking hour she existed. She had not had the luxury of being depressed. Now she sat back and had nothing but time to think and worry until they arrived.

Without meaning to, Afton let out a loud, draining sigh. Lorenz glanced in her direction, appearing to finally acknowledge she was making the trip with them. Obviously feeling guilty about leaving her out of the discussion, Lorenz reached for her hand and brought it to his lips.

"It will be another two hours before we reach your new home," Lorenz informed her. "Do you have any questions you would like to ask about the stronghold?"

"I feel like I have traveled back in time to medieval Europe, where keeps and strongholds protected the residents from barbaric hordes," Afton commented. This world continued to be so foreign to what she was used to in modern day Chicago. She struggled between wanting to return to being an oddity on Earth and trying to make a life here in the Nightshade universe with Lorenz.

"That description is not too far from the truth," Lorenz admitted. "The most important resource in this world is blood. Most vampire hives will do just about anything to capture as many humans as possible. There are more advanced settlements that treat blood more as a commodity, rather than something to kill for."

"Your father would be considered a warlord from ancient times on your planet," Drake continued. "He is one of the most powerful of his kind, probably because he is so ruthless. There is little Yorik will not do to maintain the strength of his hive."

"Including selling his daughter," Afton said under her breath.

"Actually," Drake said, "your father's handling of you has been the only vulnerable act I have ever witnessed from him. Although you will probably find this hard to believe, your father feels very deeply toward you. It would be wrong to try to compare his affection to any type of paternal examples you witnessed on Earth. We are not human and do not have human emotions."

"But, what about you and Lorenz?" Afton asked. "You both appear human, unlike the blood lusting vampires, I have lived with for almost five weeks."

"Those of us with The Creator's blood in our veins have the ability to better control our thirst," Drake answered. There had to be more to why Drake and Lorenz appeared to be human, while her father and the others could star in any creature feature horror movie.

"I have seen my father's men gorge," Afton continued, "yet they never appear human like the two of you. I saw how you cared for Shirl and then Alex's baby. There is more to your blood than you are admitting."

Before Drake could answer there was a loud explosion and the train compartment violently jolted. Afton was thrown away from Lorenz, as the carriage was ripped apart. The car pitched forward before it came to a sudden stop.

She landed hard on what had once been a chair. Pain pierced through her body. Afton looked up and was surprised to see blue sky and the sun beating down on the train wreck. The top of the train looked like it had been folded back by a can opener. She was covered with debris and dirt, but as far as she could tell, she was still in one piece. Without conscious thought, she wiggled both her fingers and toes to make sure everything was still functioning.

Dazed, she looked up at the sun in wonder, its warmth bathing her skin. How she had missed the orb she had taken for granted all of her life. Afton pushed away the minor debris that covered her body and shifted to see how Lorenz and Drake faired. All she could see was the mangled steel of the train and the planet's soil filling in where Lorenz and Drake had previously sat. Struggling to her feet, she felt a momentary twinge as her hip reacted to moving after being bruised in the collision.

"Lorenz," Afton cried. She struggled to clear the distance between where she had been thrown and where she had last seen Lorenz and Drake. Continually calling his name as she cleared away pieces of debris, her fingers dug through the soil to grab metal fragments to remove.

"Stop what you are trying to do," Lorenz called from the other side of the mess between them. "The soil is protecting us from the sun. We are going to have to wait for sunset before we can remove ourselves. Are you hurt?"

"Can you breathe?" It was a stupid question to ask. He was talking to her, so naturally he could breathe. Rational thought was too much to ask for at this point. Afton was now functioning on adrenaline and fear. Her mind was cluttered with trying to figure out how much time they had before they were buried alive and her system shutting down from shock. It was imperative she get control of herself. She needed to get help for Lorenz and Drake. There were other passengers on the train who also needed to be seen to.

"The metal structure is partially intact," Drake communicated through the mountain of debris. "As long as there is not another explosion we should be fine."

Movement from above grabbed her attention. Someone was coming to their aid. She needed to get whoever was roaming the surface to provide whatever aid possible.

"Hello," Afton called.

She squinted up and saw a figure wearing some kind of covering. Due to the brightness of the sun, Afton at first had a hard time making out what he had on. Once he got closer, she noted it almost looked like a fire retardant suit some firemen wear when they enter a burning building. How odd that this individual would be dressed in this manner.

Realization hit Afton hard. It was not a coincidence that there had been an explosion and the man wore something that would protect him from the sun and any fires that might have resulted from the train derailment. It was also clear he was coming after her. Afton looked around the wreckage for a weapon. She picked up a piece of metal that had once been part of the train's frame.

"Stay away from me," Afton cried as the man maneuvered around the mangled mess that had once been their mode of transportation. She steadied her stance as she prepared for the intruder to come at her.

"Whatever is going on, Afton," Lorenz cried out to her, "do not put up any resistance. You are not strong enough to present much of a challenge. Do what you need to survive, I will come after you."

"I don't think so," Afton responded. "My days of being the victim are over." She was not going to turn herself over without a fight, even if it meant this was her dying act. "If you want me, you are going to have to take me by force. Maybe I will be lucky enough to tear whatever you are wearing and watch the sun turn you into ash."

The man kept coming at her, unaffected by her words. Afton raised her weapon just above her head and went to stab the man in the shoulder as he came upon her. He caught her forearm as she swung the steel rod. With his other hand, he grabbed her wrist and squeezed it until she cried out in pain, dropping her weapon.

From the corner of her eye she saw his fist coming straight for her face. She heard Lorenz calling out to her before everything went black.

"Afton," Lorenz yelled, as he continued to try to free himself from the debris that had him pinned to what was left of the train's floor. He heard shuffling from the direction Afton's voice had come from earlier. In desperation, he let out an agonizing scream, helpless to save her. Even if he had been able to liberate himself from the wreckage, the Nightshade's sun would have prevented him from assisting Afton. He had felt fatigue consume his body from the close proximity to the sun's light.

"Relax, my friend," Drake said, "there is nothing we can do until the sun sets. Whoever planted the explosives has managed to retrieve what they were after. Neither of us will rest until we have Afton back."

"We should have completed the transformation before we left Yorik's stronghold." Lorenz started to second guess every decision he made in regard to Afton. "Even a half-starved vampire has more strength than Afton. She barely has enough energy to stand, she has deteriorated so much."

"As I said before, there is nothing we can do for now, Lorenz. Our time is better served in figuring out who is behind the attack and where is the most likely place they have taken the girl."

Lorenz closed his eyes and attempted to reduce the frequency his heart was beating. All he could hear was the pounding within his chest. In a matter of hours he would have the strength to lift the debris off his body and emerge from their steel and dirt prison. Drake was correct, beating himself up would not serve any productive purpose.

"Afton must have been taken by a member of The League," Lorenz reasoned. "Several members live within hours of my home. Since he did not kill her, I assume he wants her for some reason. Killing her before a gathering of the brethren would elevate his standing within the group."

"Yes," Drake said, "fortunately, it will take time to gather a large enough audience to make it worth his while. Gathering such a significant number of the society will require a great deal of communication. As soon as we are free from this mess, I can use my network of anti-League resources to discover where they are keeping Afton."

Lorenz was well aware of Drake's active opposition to the group. Lying in his own blood, helpless, Lorenz knew it was time to finally come clean with Drake about his past dealings.

"Drake, there is something you need to know." Lorenz struggled to continue with his confession. He had kept this a secret from his blood brother for centuries. It had never been his intention to ever tell Drake the truth. Images of Afton's face when she knew his involvement in the group kept appearing in his mind. The silence took on a life of its own, condemning everything he had done in his past.

"If you are going to tell me you have been a member of The League, don't bother, I already know." Drake's confession shook Lorenz to his soul. He had never let on that he knew the truth, at no point, treating him any different than he had in the past.

"How long have you known?" Curiosity got the better of Lorenz.

"Almost from the start," Drake confessed. "Do you honestly believe you were able to keep such a secret from me? I was able to use your own network against you, saving what lives I could. Had you been an active member, personally killing one of the women or their precious offspring, our relationship would have ended with that act. However, your intelligence activity allowed me to save more lives than I would have otherwise. It was a relief when you finally severed your relationship with the group and rescued Afton's mother."

Relief poured over Lorenz. He would always be stained by his membership with the group, but at least Drake had been able to save a number of lives. His actions also allowed Drake to set up his own network that would now aid in saving Afton. It was almost as if destiny had a hand in originally swaying Lorenz to join the group.

"So where do we head once the sun sets?" Lorenz inquired.

"One of my chief spies is actually stationed in your keep, we will head there as soon as we are able to travel."

Lorenz was not sure who Drake was referring to, but he would elevate the man to a higher station within his community, if he was instrumental in their saving Afton. It still amazed him that Drake had been able to use his own resources to save lives. The most precious life was now in danger.

It would be several more hours before sunset. Lorenz could only hope Afton played nice and managed to continue living until he was able to rescue her. The feral vampire within him wanted to feast on the blood of the man who had taken his woman. The blood would only be sweet, if Afton was there to share it with him.

Chapter 12

~

Her head was splitting. That was the first thought Afton had as she gained consciousness. To make matters worse, her jaw was killing her. Did the bastard hit her with his fist or a crowbar? Slowly, she opened her eyes, fearing what she would find. She was in a sparsely furnished room, not unlike many of the quarters which housed the vampires in her father's stronghold. How she wished she was back at the Venture Hive, under Yorik's protection.

Afton's hands were securely tied to the bed's headboard. The rope dug into her wrists, whoever tied the knots knew what he was doing. After pulling against the rope several times, Afton realized it was futile. Unless someone released her, the bindings were there to stay. If she continued to struggle she would end up only drawing blood, which would only incite whoever was holding her. There was not a doubt in her mind, it was a vampire.

Her eyes traveled down her body. A red lace halter camisole hugged her torso. Her eyes stopped dead on her breasts. It was not the fact she was tied to a bed that shocked her, but what she looked like in the lingerie she had been dressed in. She filled out the outfit like she had never before, even after drinking animal blood on Earth. What little of Lorenz's blood she had taken had added weight to her formerly starved frame.

"Oh, I see you have decided to finally join me," her captive said, pulling her attention away from her newly discovered body. Afton looked in the direction of the voice and was surprised to see a vampire she knew. It was the one who had come to collect Lorenz for her father. The vampire who caused her to be uneasy in her own rooms. Obviously, her instincts were correct about this monster.

"Lorenz is going to turn you into a pile of dust," Afton snarled. She was not sure how long she had been unconscious, but she knew as soon as Lorenz freed himself, he would come after her. Her job was to remain alive in the meantime. Although she did not want to alienate this creature, she also did not want to appear weak. Afton was not giving him the satisfaction of seeing her fear.

The vampire eyed the door before he once again gave Afton his full attention. "I hear half-ling blood is the sweetest ambrosia any vampire will ever experience. Let us see if that is true."

The creature came upon the bed and positioned himself over Afton. Although she struggled to free herself, it was a lost cause. She could feel the vampire's drool run down her neck as he salivated over her. Bile built in her throat in reaction to the foul being straddling her body. If she closed her eyes and thought of Lorenz, maybe she would be able to endure what was about to happen.

Fangs made contact with her skin and ravaged her throat. Vampires had the ability to compel their victims to enjoy what was being done to them. This animal did not even give her that. The venom of his bite felt like acid being pumped into the wound. Unable to stop herself, Afton screamed in agony as the vampire continued to drink from her.

The excruciating pain and the weight bearing down on her body stopped instantaneously. Within a fraction of a second of the pain stopping, she felt what only could be described as a gust of wind. Immediately after the slight breeze, she felt her body being covered with dust. Afton looked up to discover another vampire with a stake leaning over her and the other vampire's remains coating her body.

Before Afton could react, the other vampire had her untied and in his arms. He was licking her throat, as a mother cat grooms her small kittens. Although she knew he was attempting to heal her, Afton was repulsed by the action and being held by this creature. As she struggled to free herself, the vampire countered by holding her tight.

"He had no right," the vampire muttered to himself. "You are mine. He was paid to steal you from Lorenz, nothing more. I will purge the traitor's kiss and scent from your body. Come, I will bathe you, and once your blood is clean, I will make you mine."

Her delicate composition had all it could take. The stink of the other vampire was still on her and the thought of this new vampire touching her caused the bile she had been struggling with to escape. As she fell to her knees to vomit, her captor came down beside her. Like Lorenz, he held her hair back as she gagged up what little she had in her stomach. It had been criminal to compare this animal with Lorenz. While her body continued to helplessly convulse, he murmured words of affection in her ear.

After what felt like an eternity, Afton finally stopped vomiting. He brought her back into his arms and carried her from the room. She peered over his shoulder as he made his way through the structure. The halls they traveled were similar to the ones at the Venture Hive. In an attempt to garner her strength, she rested against his chest. If she could just close her eyes for a couple of minutes, she would have the stamina to fight off whatever came next.

He entered a room that looked well-lived in. It was cluttered with cast off clothing and a wealth of possessions which had not been replaced in whatever storage area they were originally housed.

Although the castle appeared to be old, it had a modern bathroom, again, not unlike her father's keep. She wondered what other human women had been victimized in these surroundings. He took her directly into the bathroom and turned on the shower. Afton so badly desired to wash, she was not bothered when the vampire peeled off the negligee she had been wearing. Nor was she disturbed when he took a cloth and started to bathe her. She was but a husk until Lorenz came to save her. She concentrated on mentally leaving her body, not caring what happened to it in the meantime.

She was herded out of the shower and wrapped in a blanket. Although she was still wet, he took her to the bed and lay her upon it. As he removed the blanket, cool air caressed her body. He crawled on top of her and buried his nose in the crook of her neck. She could feel him sniffing her and then he stopped abruptly.

He lifted himself from her body and gave her an accusing look. At this point she was beyond caring what had angered this vampire. "You smell of him," he said.

"Who?" she asked without thought.

"Lorenz, the traitor." Now that captured Afton's attention. The vampire had some type of history with Lorenz. Her curiosity was piqued. Afton was also happy she still carried Lorenz's scent after everything that had happened today. It gave her further hope she would be reunited with him.

"Why a traitor?" Afton imagined this creature was a member of The League, since Lorenz had dropped from the group and ultimately worked on its demise.

"Lorenz took what was originally mine. The power I would have possessed killing your mother. I will drain you of every drop of that traitor's blood once I have killed him. Only with his death will I truly possess you."

"What do you have planned?" It was obvious this vampire liked to show how clever he thought he was. If Afton could learn of his plans, perhaps she would be able to throw a wrench or two into them. She could also try to reach Lorenz telepathically. Afton was not sure what distance their mind connection covered.

A truly evil smile crossed the vampire's face. It was almost as if he could read her mind and was mocking her. "It will not be hard to lead Lorenz here and kill him. Maybe I will do it slowly and you can watch. Once I have purged his blood from your body, I will take you right in front of him. It is time I live up to my new name."

She was not going to give him the satisfaction of asking what he was now calling himself. It was curious, he seemed more interested in his own false vanity than her naked body before him. Afton figured when the time was right, she could use that in her favor.

"I have procured one of your former servants from your father's stronghold. You treat me right, she will come to no harm. Now ask me."

She knew what he wanted and she was now forced to comply. "What is your name?"

"Malice."

Chapter 13

It would be hard to determine who was more in a foul mood, him or his visitor from the Troyk universe? The contingent arrived about a week after he and Drake liberated themselves from the train wreckage and made their way to his home. Koel had met his soul mate and was disappointed she had not fallen immediately into his arms.

Lorenz was frustrated that Afton was not with him, where she belonged. The big difference was that Koel's soul mate was not in mortal danger, where Lorenz's was. It took him by surprise when he thought of Afton in those terms. He knew there had been a bond between them, but had not considered a legend was coming true.

Whoever took her had covered his tracks well. All of Drake's resources had come up dry when inquiries were first made. Days went by without any concrete information. He thought he would go mad, not knowing if Afton was alive or dead. Slowly information started to trickle in. Finally word about activity in a once deserted keep, not far from his own home, started to circulate.

"Is the intelligence good?" Koel asked. Even though he was preoccupied with his soul mate, Lorenz was impressed with Koel's tactical mind. He asked all the questions Lorenz had thought of and additional ones as well. Koel seemed to look at a plan from different perspectives, some of which Lorenz had not considered. When Koel discovered a new angle on the planned rescue, Lorenz beat himself up for not thinking of it himself.

Once Drake discovered Alex and the baby were in good health, he too was able to properly concentrate on the matter at hand. All their efforts focused on saving Afton from her kidnappers. It had been a high risk and daring way to extract her from his side. If any more explosives had been used, everyone in their train compartment would have died, being blown to bits. Lorenz was not pleased Afton was taken by someone able to pull off such a daring mission.

"The double agent has been totally reliable in the past," Drake responded. "His cover story within The Society's organization is beyond reproach. We sacrificed a woman early on to solidify his standing. Her rescue had been a lost cause, so we used her loss to the best of our ability. I am not proud of what we did, but this way her death means something."

Koel looked at Drake long and hard. "If we do this right, the two of you will not have to be involved. If Afton is exactly where your contact says she will be, we can get her out in the light of day."

Lorenz rubbed his eyes with the balls of his fingers. The first intelligence they had received smelled like a trap and had been exactly that. The double agent had come forward and debunked what they had learned before they were stupid enough to take action.

Now the question was whether the latest information was trustworthy. The vampire had offered to be held hostage while the Troyk warriors freed Afton to prove what he said was legitimate. Every instinct Lorenz had, told him the plan was going to work. He had to have faith in his own feelings and let the plan move forward.

"As soon as we are free of the settlement, I will open a portal which will return us here." Shirl finally joined the discussion. Her relationship with Drake had changed when Alex's baby entered the picture. It was clear she was weary of Drake's interest in the child.

Lorenz could not figure out if it was jealousy or true concern on Shirl's part. Regardless, he was happy the powerful crystal telepath was willing to risk her own life to rescue Afton. It was reassuring that if the plan went terribly wrong, Shirl would be able to open a portal directly into the room where they currently sat. No one wanted the Troyk involvement in the rescue known, unless it was the only way to save Afton and the rest of the team.

"It is a go then," Koel stated. "Tomorrow when the sun reaches its zenith, we will rescue your woman."

Lorenz did not object to how Koel referred to Afton. Once he got her back, he would make sure what the Troyk warrior said was more than just words. They would complete the joining and would finally be together. That vision he continually saw when he looked at Afton, would finally be her true self. Tomorrow's operation just had to be successful for that to happen.

⁘

Afton leaned back in her chair and stared at the sun through the purple filter. This was her reward for letting Malice touch her. Somehow he had managed to find Lenore and bring her here. For all his frightening words, Malice had not harmed her servant or taken either of their blood. Lorenz's blood continued to work miracles, as her body slowly transformed. Her captor foolishly believed it was his touch that was causing the half-ling to change before his eyes. Afton thought it was not prudent to tell him differently.

She had mastered the ability to mentally leave her body whenever she was forced to be with Malice. He daily explored her body, marveling at what he had brought about. How she longed to be free of this place and back with Lorenz.

Once they completed the joining, Afton could not wait to see what happened. She looked at her body through a scientist's eye as Malice touched the new flesh that had been added to her frame. The clothes she wore had to be replaced daily as she put on weight. Her outfits were skin tight, in order for Malice to see evidence of *his* handiwork when they were not alone. It had only been a week since she had been here, but already she figured she had put on twenty pounds.

Relief had consumed her when Malice had reported his earlier plan to trap Lorenz had failed. The fool had even looked at that as a sign he should not capture Lorenz until she had finished the transformation Malice thought he had initiated. Afton knew Lorenz would not rest until he successfully liberated her.

The man who held her captive was delusional. He would take credit for everything around him, even if he had no part in what she was evolving into. Malice laughed at how amazed Lorenz would be at his own failure to join with the woman given to him by contract. Malice would throw in Lorenz's face what he had been able to do. After he was done showing her off to Lorenz, Malice would bring together The Society and show them what was possible with a worthy half-ling. That thought scared Afton and she prayed Lorenz would rescue her before that happened.

There was another reason she prayed Lorenz and Drake would save her soon. When Malice believed her transformation was complete, he would then free her of Lorenz's blood so they could finally be together. He did not elaborate on what that meant, but she did not think it was something she was going to enjoy, let alone live through.

She moved her gaze over to Lenore, who was planting flowers. They were at the west end of the keep where the only open area within the compound existed. If it was not for her hour in the sun daily, Afton would have gone mad by now. Fortunately, Malice liked the color her time in the garden added to her cheeks. Each day she enjoyed the sun before submitting herself to Malice's inspection.

Afton closed her eyes and concentrated on the here and now. She would not ruin her hour of happiness every day, by thinking about what would happen once she was led back inside and to Malice's chamber. The different flowers blooming in the garden ran through her mind, as her face was warmed by the sun.

Her peace was rocked by a small explosion. Instantly her thoughts raced back to the train wreck, as metal and dirt debris washed over her. She was gently shaken and she opened her eyes to see Shirl standing before her.

"We need to escape the purple tarp before the vampires come out to investigate the blast," Shirl said as she grabbed her hand and helped her to her feet. Together they ran side by side toward the hole in the wall the explosion had created.

Before she had a chance to tell Shirl they also needed to rescue Lenore, Afton noted the woman was running beside Shirl's soul mate Starc. They quickly made it to the rubble and slowed their strides as they navigated through the broken stone and past the purple barrier. The unfiltered sun bathed her face, finally free of Malice's keep.

For the first time since arriving in the Nightshade universe, Afton got to see what the surface of this parallel world looked like. As far as she was concerned, she might as well be on Earth. They were in a small clearing and made their way into a forest. One by one they quickly walked through the woods until they entered a beautiful meadow.

Shirl walked away from the group and Afton noticed her amethyst glowed. After what happened on Earth, Afton was not surprised to see a wall of displaced air opening on the other side of where Shirl stood. It was the most beautiful sight she had ever seen.

"This is one portal I am sure you will want to step through," Starc said, as he came beside her.

"Is it back to Earth or Lorenz?" Afton asked.

"Where do you want it to lead?" Starc had such a serious look on his face. At that point she knew that if it did not lead to where Afton asked to go, he would have Shirl open another portal.

"You know," Afton said in wonder, "I do not even have to think about it. It needs to take me back to Lorenz."

Shirl came up to her and asked, "Are you sure?" It was evident she had opened a portal back to Chicago, Evanston to be exact.

"Look at me, Shirl," Afton replied. "I only took a little of Lorenz's blood and I feel like a different woman. Once we complete the joining, I will no longer have the sickly half-ling body I have been imprisoned in."

The crystal telepath looked at Afton and considered her words. Another man came up to them, he resembled Starc. She figured they were brothers or perhaps cousins. "Open another portal, Shirl. She belongs with her soul mate, as you belong with yours and I will one day be with mine." He came up to her and extended his hand. "I am Koel, by the way."

"Thank you, Koel," Afton said. She would have been heartbroken if she ended up being stranded on Earth. With everything that had happened since entering the Nightshade universe, she knew she belonged here. Despite Lorenz's past, Afton had been destined to be with him.

As Shirl was directed to do, one air displacement closed and another one opened. It happened so quickly, if she had not been staring at the portal, Afton would have missed the change. Her future was on the other side of the event horizon.

Afton stood before the portal. The last time she had been mentally manipulated to walk through and enter the Nightshade universe. This time she did not have to be coerced. She stepped through the portal to a man who would transform her body. For the first time in her life, she desperately wanted another being's love.

Malice rammed his fist through the flimsy screen he had erected to provide Afton privacy after each of their sessions. His hands longed to touch her and he knew of no other way to release his pent-up frustration. She had become his obsession. Her guards were late delivering her once again. How had she manipulated them this time to forestall the inevitable? Had he not given her sunshine and space for her to recover her sensibilities?

It was his time with the half-ling which brought upon his new zest for life. All those years he had enjoyed hunting down women who carried the genetic marker led him to this moment. Now he wanted to create, rather than destroy. Their being together was inevitable, she just had to come to terms with it. Perhaps she would warm up to him after Lorenz no longer breathed and his blood was removed from her veins.

She was changing before his eyes. True, it was Lorenz's blood that had started her metamorphosis- but it was Malice's touch molding her into what she was slowly becoming. He could almost hear the little sounds escaping from her mouth as his hand caressed her body.

How he longed to capture those moans with his mouth. Once again, his cock wanted to be more than just a bystander. Although she struggled to control her body's reaction to him, eventually she would be crying out with pleasure when they were finally together. None of his dreams would become reality until he dealt with Lorenz.

A small group of guards entered the room and fell to their knees. "Mercy," the guard in front cried, "the half-ling escaped through no fault of our own. There was an explosion that destroyed the north wall of the exterior courtyard. The human servants we sent to investigate reported she was no longer in the confines of the keep. We sent men into the woods behind the wall. That is all we can do until the sun sets and it is safe to search for her."

Malice looked at the hole he had created on the screen and knew his hands were not done destroying what was around him. "Which of you will pay the price for failing to safeguard my property?"

The men looked at each other, waiting for one among them to make the supreme sacrifice. Their failure would be paid and there would be one less among them to consume what little blood was available. It was not an uncommon occurrence to handle a botched assignment in such a fashion.

A vampire in the rear stepped forward. "It was you who allowed her to venture into the daylight, making it impossible for us to properly guard her. I am tired of this existence and will pay the ultimate price."

"Then you among those who failed will be the only who will live." Malice had exacted the perfect punishment for the creature. He was the only one among the men on their knees who might one day be salvageable. "Lock him in the dungeon and provide him no blood for a week. After that time, he may return to his normal duties." He motioned to the rest of the disgraced guards. "Give whatever blood you can extract from their worthless hides to the new recruits."

Malice had no desire to share in the bounty of their blood. It was only Afton's he now craved. He doubted it was still the ambrosia half-ling blood, but he knew it would be the sweetest thing he had ever tasted. Soon, he would finally taste her blood as he stood over Lorenz's ashes.

Alone once again, he considered what had occurred. Perhaps it was for the best he temporarily lost the girl. His enemy would complete the transformation ceremony and then he would reclaim his property thereafter. Already he could feel her fuller breasts, his fingers tingled in response.

He called one of the black haired surrogates he had selected. While he was gentle to Afton, Malice was able to relieve the needs his body had for blood and release. Slowly he undressed, anticipating what was to come. He would gorge on each of her doubles until his true mate was once again in his control. Afton would be punished for what she was forcing him to do to these women.

Chapter 14

~

"Will you sit and stop your constant pacing!" Drake demanded.

Lorenz knew he was driving his friend crazy, but he could not help the anxiety that continued to consume him. Never before had he cared for another being the way he felt for Afton. It was driving him insane not knowing how she faired. If anything happened to her, he was not sure he wanted to continue living. Every moment, that passed without the portal opening was like a stake driven deeper into his heart.

The air before him shimmered and a woman walked through. At first he did not recognize her and then was shocked when he realized Afton stood before him. The remainder of the rescue party exited the portal, but Lorenz only had eyes for the woman he had been tearing himself apart over.

Standing there like a fool, Lorenz soaked up the vision who stood before him. She must have gained twenty pounds in the time they had been separated. The little blood they had exchanged should not have caused such a drastic transformation unless they were truly soul mates. These were the thoughts he would have to explore later, for now he wanted to take Afton into his arms.

Reluctantly Lorenz stepped forward, a part of him afraid he was dreaming and once he touched her, she would disappear. He fell to his knees before her and wrapped his arms around her waist. Lorenz allowed his head to momentarily rest on her fleshy abdomen. She was no longer skin and bones, but a more filled out woman.

"Thank The Creator," Lorenz said to no one in particular, "you are safe." He turned to address the people responsible for Afton's rescue. "How can I ever repay you?"

Shirl came forward. "You helped to rescue Candy, no payment is required. Besides, I cannot help but feel partly responsible for Afton being here to begin with. I had not planned to return her to you, however. The portal I originally opened would have returned her to Earth. It was Afton's choice to be with you."

Lorenz stood, still holding Afton close. He looked into her eyes, hoping to see some type of affection reflected in her gaze. With everything the girl had been through, she chose to return to him. Her gaze was full of tears, her pupils were partly dilated. Apprehension was reflected in her glance. He knew he had to reassure her she was safe and above everything else, wanted.

"Every waking hour," Lorenz pledged, "I will dedicate myself to your safety and happiness. If I learned anything these past seven days, I have no future without you."

A sob escaped from Afton, as she wrapped her arms around his neck and rested her head against his chest. Lorenz rubbed her back as she released tears of relief. He held her tightly as her body shook.

"We will leave now," Starc stated. "Drake, Shirl and I will return in four days to take you to Benko Jarlyn. It is still his desire to forge an alliance with you against Yorik. Make sure you have the crystals we discussed when we return."

Lorenz watched in amusement as Drake started to approach Shirl and her soul mate intercepted him. The crystal telepath threw a smirk in Drake's direction. The woman was fearless. She had been aware of Drake's manipulation of the special bond that existed between her and her soul mate.

"Take care of Alex and her child," Drake countered, knowing those words would get a reaction from Shirl.

"It is my mission in life to care for my friend and her child," Shirl spit out at him. "That includes keeping them away from you and your warped powers and sense of entitlement."

Afton shifted in his arms. She brought her mouth to his ear and whispered, "You are enjoying their sparring, but I figure I can bring you more pleasure than they can. It is time we finish the joining."

She had barely finished her sentence when she was rocketed into Lorenz's arms. As he carried her from the room Afton shouted, "Thank you." There was no question, she owed her life to these people. Afton knew she would see Shirl, Starc, and Koel again. For now, however, she wanted to be alone with Lorenz. It was thoughts of a future with Lorenz that got her through her time with Malice. She reveled in his frustration when his plans to kill Lorenz were stymied.

He carried her along with stone walkways, not unlike the ones in her father's keep. The few servants they passed seemed healthy and hearty. Lenore told her humans and vampires lived in harmony in Lorenz's settlement. She was grateful the woman was now safely here.

Lorenz stopped and shifted her in his arms as he opened the door they stood before. After they entered, Lorenz kicked the door shut behind him. She felt a sense of loss when he placed her on her own two feet.

They were in a large chamber. Purple light flooded the room from windows on the far side. Although she wanted to explore the area with her eyes, they kept coming back to the bed which dominated the room. Ultimately, thoughts of being with Lorenz had sustained her through Malice's explorations, Afton just did not know if she could relax and give herself to the man before her.

Lorenz drew a knife from his boot and placed it against his neck. Afton gasped as he cut a gash across his carotid artery. Her father had told her it was the most powerful blood a vampire's body produced. Crimson liquid quickly escaped from the cut. His action was enough of an invitation for Afton to place her lips against the wound and drink.

Fireworks went off behind her closed eyes. The blood she consumed burned through her veins, bringing her pleasure beyond description. Her heart rate increased as the organ pumped the life affirming blood throughout her body. Tendons seemed to stretch, as muscles strengthened in reaction to the nourishment. Her scalp burned as her fine, limp hair transformed into thicker, curly strands. The seams of her tight dress started to pop as her body filled out in reaction to Lorenz's blood.

As her body continued to soak in Lorenz's sustenance, she could feel him stripping the ruined dress from her body. His hands caressed her as she continued to drink. Her skin absorbed his touch, as her body continued to take in his life-force.

A sense of near gluttony started to overwhelm her. Instinctively she knew she needed to stop drinking from her mate and feed him instead. "Take my blood," she pleaded. They would not complete the joining until Lorenz had his fill.

Within a heartbeat, Lorenz was at her throat and bit into the tender flesh. Unlike her kidnapper's bite, Lorenz's capture of her neck brought about near-orgasmic pleasure. She grabbed his head and brought him closer. He would not be able to release her until she was ready.

She whimpered when Lorenz stopped pulling against her artery. He lifted her, as she released her hold on his head. Lorenz started to carry her to the bed when she saw a full size mirror out of the corner of her eye.

"Stop," she cried, "I want to see what I look like." She had felt her body change as she drank, but she wanted to see the physical evidence of the transformation.

She stood before the mirror and stared in disbelief. The woman before her had ample breasts, powerful legs, and a perfect hourglass figure. Her hair was thick and shone in the lavender rays coming from the window. Although she had felt her body change, Afton still could not believe the woman she saw reflected in the mirror was her.

Although she stood naked, she was not embarrassed as Lorenz also gazed at her. He came up, brushed back the hair from her left shoulder, and started to caress her neck with his lips. Afton turned and placed her lips against his.

Lorenz deepened the kiss and directed her toward the bed. They continued on their journey until the back of her legs came against the mattress. Grabbing her waist, Lorenz lifted her onto the bed and covered her with his body. Afton was drowning in his touch.

"*Let me enter you and we will complete the joining,*" Lorenz communicated to her telepathically. There was something so personal in the unspoken communication through a pathway that only the two of them shared. He touched her brain the way he touched her body, a touch so delicate, meant only for her.

The meaning of his words finally hit her mind and she started to panic. Afton had no idea what completing the joining would mean. Her body had transformed beyond what she ever considered possible. What happened if the transformation turned her into someone she did not know any more?

Instinctively she leveraged the same telepathic channel Lorenz had used earlier. "*Stop!*"

He ceased kissing her almost immediately upon her cry. Lorenz looked into her eyes, questioning what had happened that had stopped the chemistry they had brewing between them. Afton knew she was in control of what would happen next.

"I am not ready yet," she told him.

Lorenz appeared startled by her confession. After everything she had been through, how could he be surprised she was not ready to take their relationship to the next level? The bonding was more than a physical act, but a mental joining as well.

Realization dawned in Lorenz's gaze. "Did he take you against your will?"

This was one conversation she did not want to have. She had a hard enough time dealing with everything that had happened, the idea of putting them into words to explain to Lorenz was beyond her capacity. Regardless of what she thought she was capable of at this point, she needed to answer his question. At least she could relieve his anxiety related to whether she had been raped.

"He violated me with his touch and his threats. The monster was not going to consummate our relationship until you were dead and your blood was exorcised from my body." She choked out the words. How she was able to verbalize everything was a mystery to her.

Lorenz rolled off her and wrapped her body in the bed linens. He covered her with such care, as if he was trying to erase what had happened to her. Her emotional scars were not going to be so easily dismissed.

"Can you just hold me?" Afton asked, her voice just over a whisper. She would be shattered if he left her at this point.

To her relief, Lorenz pulled her into his body. Heat penetrated the sheet which cocooned her. A sense of home consumed Afton, a feeling she never thought she would ever feel. If she could, she would freeze this moment. It was as perfect as she had ever experienced. Fear of what she would morph into once the claiming was completed crept into her peaceful mood.

Chapter 15

～

Afton tugged the brush through her hair for the billionth time. If nature had transformed her into the most of her body's potential, why hadn't she been given tangle-free hair? The thick curly hair was a tangled mess. It had a life of its own, its mission to drive her insane. Every time she thought she had tamed it, wisps of hair escaped from their confinement. Afton was about to throw her brush in a fit of frustration when Lenore grabbed her wrist.

"Let me help you with that," Lenore said in a calming voice. She took the brush and gently ran it through Afton's hair. Lenore worked through the snags with the skill of a seasoned beautician. She wrapped the unyielding strands and strategically applied pins until she stood back and admired her handiwork. Afton stared in wonder at the coiffed masterpiece before her.

"Wow," Afton said in wonder, "you are a miracle worker."

"I am nothing of the kind," Lenore replied. "To survive in this world, I needed to have a lot of patience. It is a trait all who dwell in the Nightshade universe should possess." Afton figured it was Lenore's way of telling her *she* needed to display more of the talent in the future.

She continued to stare at her reflection, considering Lenore's words. Her week with Malice had been nothing compared to what Lenore had suffered at the hands of her father and the other vampires. Afton was pleased Lenore was here now with her, safe from further vampire violence.

"Where did they take you after we were separated?" Afton asked. She had always wondered where she had disappeared to. Guilt consumed her, since she would have been indirectly responsible for any punishment the woman had been subjected to.

"Originally I feared I would be given to the collective to feed on. Few survive the feeding attack of multiple vampires. As I was being led away, a lone vampire took possession of me. I was taken to the stronghold we just escaped from and was pretty much left alone. It was not long before we were reunited."

For some reason she could not comprehend, Malice had rescued Lenore and kept her safe to ultimately become Afton's servant again. He had shown her consideration, even Lorenz had not. Everything about that creature confused her. There was no question he meant her harm, but at the same time he planned for her comfort.

"Your new clothes will be ready soon." Lenore's voice drew Afton away from her thoughts of Malice. It would be nice to wear real clothes again. Afton was currently wrapped in a robe, all other clothing no longer fit her transformed body. She could not even enjoy the clothing Darden had brought from Earth. "I never believed the fables of vampire soul mates until I saw you this morning."

"What stories?" Afton inquired.

"Your soul mate and Drake were turned by the original vampire. I do not know if he had a name, he is usually referred to as The Creator. After countless millennia of surviving, a woman fell through a portal and captivated the original one. It is said once they joined, The Creator would transform into what nature had originally planned. The couple left before the transformation, wanting to be free of this world before The Creator lost the ability to travel between universes."

"But surely other vampires and half-lings have shared blood as Lorenz and I have done."

"Very few half-lings survive to an age when the joining can be performed," Lenore confessed. "Stories never mention the extent of how much Lorenz's blood caused you to change. There is talk that you are soul mates. We are all anxious to see what will happen after the two of you make love."

Afton blushed. Love did not factor into the equation when it came to the two of them. She was not sure how she felt about Lorenz, lust certainly factored into those feelings. His bite and his blood did wonderful things to her body. Despite the train episode, she felt safe in his presence.

"What do the legends say about what happens to the half-ling and vampire after they make love?" There were a number of factors preventing her from jumping into the sack with Lorenz, fear of what they would evolve into was on the top of the list.

"It is said they will stop feeding from others," Lenore shared. "Their need for each other will result in a compulsion not to take anyone else's blood." After what she had experienced drinking from Lorenz, Afton already could not imagine taking nourishment any other way. Normal blood had not fed her hungry cells, while animal blood had managed to barely sustain her all these years. Lorenz's life-force was like rocket fuel for her starving body.

"What else?"

Lenore drew closer, ready to share the greatest secret of all. "A mated vampire, according to legend, can walk in the sun." Afton had always been sensitive to the rays of the sun. Perhaps once she had intercourse with Lorenz, she would be able to lie in the sun in a bikini. She knew her transformed body would fill one out quite nicely. In the grand scheme of things it seemed rather inconsequential, but it was something she had always longed for. She had always been depressed when the other girls clad in the newest beach fashions headed to the Lake Michigan beaches.

"Do the legends tell of anything negative stemming from the final joining?" There had to be a terrible consequence, everything Lenore had shared seemed too good to be true.

"They are just stories, Afton. You will not know the true extent of what you evolve into until you have truly been with Lorenz. It is not my place, but if I were you, I would want every advantage to survive in this universe. I should check on your clothing. Is there anything I can get you in the meantime?"

"No," Afton answered, disappointment evident in her short reply. She knew she should not be taking her frustrations out on her servant. Fortunately, Lenore did not take offense to how she had been addressed.

One thing was clear, Lenore was right about being all she could be to survive in this universe. Just sharing blood with Lorenz had made her healthier than she had been in her life. If the stories were true, she would be a fool not to take the next step with Lorenz. Fear of a variety of things were stopping her from having sex with the man she longed to be with. Afton needed to conquer her doubts and do what needed to be done. The only question was how she was going to seduce him.

"I would love to wipe that stupid grin off your face," Lorenz literally growled at Drake. He was in a terrible mood, the least his friend could do was mask his own happiness. It was remarkable how often his mood had soured as of late, all related to the half-ling who had taken over his bedroom.

Drake seemed to get as much enjoyment out of sparring verbally with the crystal telepath as he did drinking her blood. The child in the chameleon's womb seemed the panacea for anything that had once bothered his blood brother. Only time would tell if anything would develop between Drake and the child.

How he wished he had some kind of miracle salve to lessen the effect Afton had on him. His body literally ached for her. When she had rejected being with him, Lorenz was crushed. It was an odd reaction for a vampire to have. The girl was bringing out the human he had not been in several millennia. He understood why she had stopped their lovemaking, but he still could not help taking it personally.

"You should just bed her and get it over with," Drake said. "Seduce the girl. The poor thing has been through so much, she is not going to willingly give herself to a vampire. Make her forget what you are and everything she has been through since she arrived in our world. There are ways of turning off the female brain."

How simple Drake made everything sound. He was not sure what nightmares Afton suffered and he did not want to add to her waking terrors. Compelling her to make love to him seemed wrong. Lorenz wanted Afton to give herself to him body and soul, without a moment's hesitation. Her brain had already been manipulated to get her into the Nightshade Universe by mind control telepaths. He did not want that particular violation between them.

"Perhaps I should send her back to Ginkgo Terra when Shirl returns," Lorenz confessed. He struggled with what was best for the girl. Perhaps her spending some time where she felt safe and was in no danger from The League was the right thing to do.

"I have never known you to be a quitter," Drake confessed. "That girl belongs here and with you. Rumors are circulating among the servants about the two of you being soul mates. Now is not the time to grow an idiotic conscience.

Besides, I do not want to give Shirl the satisfaction of returning her to Earth. With Afton here, my crystal telepath will continue to check on her well-being."

"What of the child?"

"It will be a number of years before that girl will be old enough for me to determine what we may have together. In the meantime, there is much enjoyment to be had playing with the beautiful blonde."

"You are a sick bastard."

Drake laughed. "I am a vampire. Unlike you, I still have a sense of humor and a delightfully warped sense of fun. I plan to milk the future Troyk ruler and his followers for everything I can. Then I will claim what may be mine."

Those words brought Lorenz back to his dilemma, the girl he desired beyond comprehension. Every part of his being cried out for her blood and to take possession of her once and for all. There was not a doubt in his mind, she was his soul mate. It was not the promise of the sun and other powers he would gain by being with her that drove him. Ultimately, it was the man he once was, longing to be with the woman who had been created strictly for him.

"Would you imagine that soul mates between vampire and half-ling would possess some kind of psychic bond, like between Troyk soul mates? How did you find the channel between Shirl and Starc?" Although Lorenz had already communicated with Afton telepathically, he wanted to know if he had leveraged the soul mate bond.

Drake seemed to be considering his answer. Sometimes things came naturally and putting them into words was not an easy task to perform. It was not unlike his feelings for Afton.

"Our shared blood has opened a link between the two of us," Drake finally said. "It is what we use to communicate telepathically. That same link causes us to know when the other is in danger. You merely need to concentrate and find what binds you with Afton. Stop calling and thinking of her as a half-ling, but as your soul mate."

Lorenz was ashamed he continued to label Afton. Perhaps that was one of the things that was holding her back from giving herself to him. If Drake had been able to pick it up, Afton must be aware of it as well.

One of Drake's spies entered the great hall and handed a note to him. Drake read it and his expression changed to one of seriousness. It was a look

Lorenz seldom saw reflected on his blood brother's face. The message must have contained troubling news.

"You need to complete the joining with Afton immediately," Drake said.

"What has happened? What did the note contain?"

"The vampire who had taken Afton has been identified," Drake responded. "You go to Afton and I will call for reinforcements, we need Frazour."

Drake and Lorenz were two of five blood brothers. Frazour was the most lethal of them all, as well as the most feral. There were times he was more of an animal than a man. Things had to be dire for Drake to call in the worst of them.

"Who are we dealing with, Drake?"

"Go to Afton. I need to know what you evolve into before I call the others. Your main concern now is Afton. We will meet after you have completed the joining. She will be one of us and we will need her at full strength if we are all going to survive this."

Chapter 16

~

Lorenz made his way to his chamber, his mind consumed with trying to figure out who had been behind Afton's abduction. Why Drake would not confide in him was troubling, as well as his desire to bring Frazour in to help. It had been hundreds of years since he had seen that particular blood brother. As far as he was concerned, he could easily go a couple more centuries without having to deal with that animal.

Everything he had been thinking about was lost to him as soon as he entered his bedroom and saw Afton. She was in a red lace dress that left little to the imagination. The material barely covered her breasts and it was clear she was not wearing a bra. The hemline was short and showed off her long, now muscular legs, to their advantage. His mouth watered as he approached her.

Afton raised her arm, gesturing for him to stop. Whatever game she was playing, Lorenz did not like it. He wanted this woman in his arms now and he would make quick work of removing the tantalizing outfit she wore. True, he was going to destroy it, but he would have another made for her.

Battling his own desire, he stopped as she had indicated. He watched in fascination as she lifted the material resting on her shoulders. Her hands gathered up the delicate fabric as she slowly raised the dress and pulled it over her head. She stood before him, naked as the day she was born. The transformation had given her perfectly shaped breasts and ample hips. He would not be feeling bone as he touched her, but soft, womanly flesh.

Without a sound she walked toward him. Her fingers brushed his lips, indicating she did not want him to speak. For some reason, he had not reached out and brought her into his arms. He stood perfectly still as her finger outlined his lips. She barely touched him, but she was driving him mad. Then it dawned on him, she was trying to seduce him. Here he had been concerned how he was going to do the same to her. A wave of tenderness cooled his body, giving him the control to withstand Afton's touch, until the time was right for them to be joined.

"Do not touch me until I give you permission," Afton instructed. "I am not sure how vampires make love, but I have dreamed about this my whole life, so we are doing things my way." There was a confidence in her voice that was extremely sexy. If it was possible his cock managed to get harder, it would take all his self-control to honor her request.

She started to unbutton his shirt and gently pulled it out from his pants. Her hands skimmed his chest as she pushed the material off his body. He shook his arms to release the shirt's grasp on his wrists. Afton hovered over his chest, as a hummingbird ready to collect nectar from a flower.

She came in closer and started to caress his upper body with her lips, her ample breasts brushed against him. Friction caused by her nipples rubbing against his flesh, caused them to harden, in reaction he let out a deep guttural moan. If she did not release him from his slacks soon, he would have to take control away from her.

As if hearing about his need, Afton unbuttoned his pants. She did not fumble in her attempt, but with skilled fingers, she completed releasing him from his bindings. His erect member brushed against her skin, but she seemed in no hurry to let the little general have his way. Lorenz stepped out of his pants, now as naked as she was.

She stepped back and devoured him with her eyes. If she was getting half the pleasure he was examining her body, Afton was euphoric. "Turn around," she ordered, "slowly." Lorenz was more than willing to grant her request, especially if she was going to reciprocate.

When he completed his rotation, he motioned with his finger for her to give him the same consideration. She smiled as her eyes left his hand and returned to his face. Without hesitation, Afton slowly turned. Her backside was as beautiful as the front. There was a new kind of grace in how she moved.

If he had the freedom to touch her, he was not sure where he would have started. His fingers ached to caress her beautiful shoulder blades, the indentation of the small of her back, or the globes of her perfectly rounded derriere. He fisted his hands to restrain his need to touch her.

When she finished her rotation, she walked toward him and placed her lips on his. He immediately opened to take her tongue into his mouth. The kiss deepened as if they were both starving for the kiss. "Oh hell, so much for slow. I want your hands all over me and your cock inside me." Afton literally jumped on top of him, as their lips continued to ravish each other.

Lorenz navigated them to the bed. Although he would have happily taken her on the rug, Lorenz wanted Afton's first time to be on a soft, comfortable surface. As his hands explored her body and his lips continued to lavish kisses upon Afton, Lorenz searched for the psychic channel which existed between them.

He wanted to telepathically make love to her, as his body did the physical work. This was going to be a caring assault with every tool in his arsenal. After he made love to her as a man, he would let the vampire free to complete the joining. It was the least he could do to make this special for Afton.

He laid her flat on her back and explored her body with his hands. Every inch of her deserved to be worshiped. She made little whimpering sounds as he massaged her breasts. When be brought one of her nipples into his mouth, she let loose a guttural moan. The tip of her breast further hardened as his tongue played with it. As he continued to make love to her breasts, Afton's hands roamed every inch of his body she could reach. When she finally made it to his erect member, he grabbed her hand.

"*You will unman me,*" he communicated telepathically. "*Although I am a vampire, this is the first time since I was turned that I feel human again. The control I have had since turning is lost to me at the moment. There will be other times you can explore that particular part of my anatomy, but for now let it be.*" When Lorenz released her hands, she brought them to his hips and dug her fingers into his flesh.

"Take me now, before I come without you," Afton cried. "I want us to climax together."

Lorenz already had been exploring her upper thighs, he was strategically located to follow through with her request. He took one finger and entered her warm, inviting body. Afton further spread her legs, giving him better access to her sex. His finger was already covered with her juices as he brought a second finger into her core. She shifted her legs and wrapped them around his waist.

He entered her slowly, allowing her to adjust to his size. Lorenz took her lips as he tore through the membrane he knew would be present. Afton barely flinched as he drove the rest of the way into her welcoming body. He drove in and out of her, with a frequency he never attained before. That driving action, not only fed the urgency of their bodies, but the cells of his body as only blood had done so before.

"*Do you feel that?*" he asked, almost believing it was his imagination and he needed her to confirm that was the case.

"Hell, yeah!" Afton cried out, her breathing had quickened and she was almost panting. "*Legend said we would only feed off each other in the future, I just thought it meant blood.*" She shared that last bit with him through their soul mate channel. It was doubtful his soul mate could finish a sentence orally at this point.

He continued to make love to her until they were both sated. Together they reached a shared orgasm, which was unlike anything he had experienced. Their feeding and intercourse was now one and the same. It was humbling to realize that nature had found a way to get the one woman who could fulfill his every need to him somehow. He certainly was not going to give Yorik the credit.

Their bodies were covered with a reddish sweat, excreting the excess blood they generated. He turned over on his side and took Afton with him. Lorenz wanted to explain what happened before Afton discovered it on her own. He liked when she screamed with passion and did not want to hear her scream in horror, once she saw the blood.

Afton lay in Lorenz's arms, totally exhausted. She knew it was a cliché, but he had rocked her world with the sex and his ability to touch her soul. As her body cooled, Afton concentrated on bringing down her heartbeat and controlling her breathing. "Is that how we are going to feed in the future?" Wouldn't that be amazing!

"Based on how I feel, I believe that is the case." The idea of doing that every night and whenever he desired her, was beyond anything she had ever imagined or hoped for. "I never believed in any of the ridiculous stories I had heard over the years, but now I am a believer. Unfortunately, I did not pay attention, so I am not sure what else we have to look forward to. There is just one side effect you should know about."

"What?" Just when she thought she had gotten her heart rate under control, Lorenz's words caused it to skyrocket.

"The exertion caused us to sweat, but the feeding aspect also caused the excess blood to also leave our bodies."

Afton was in such a state of euphoria, it took a couple of moments for Lorenz's words to sink in. She shot up to a sitting position and examined her body and the bedsheets. After all the blood she had been exposed to, as well as drinking, she thought there was nothing about it that would surprise her. But finding herself wrapped in blood stained sheets after making love totally freaked her out. Afton launched herself out of bed and ran toward the bathroom.

She had barely stepped into the cascading shower when Lorenz was right behind her. They had shared a shower before, but last time she was fully dressed. Afton went into his arms and welcomed his kiss.

"*You are never showering again without me.*" She loved how he was able to communicate with her without breaking the kiss. He grabbed a sponge and started to wash the blood from her skin. It was foolish to be grossed out by the blood that had been a bi-product of their new feeding routine. Once they were better able to control their body's creation of blood when they made love, it would hopefully stop escaping from their pores after they were done.

Unlike last time, her thick curly hair had started to weigh down on her, now that it was wet. "I am going to cut this damn hair," she complained. "It's going to take poor Lenore hours to get out all the tangles."

Lorenz grabbed a bottle and poured some of the creamy liquid onto her scalp. "I have the same problem, love, just a lot less of it." Afton leaned back her head as Lorenz massaged the conditioner into her scalp and then through her hair. She never realized how applying a hair product could be so sensual. To hell with her hair, her body wanted his attention!

"Make love to me again," Afton commanded. She could not get enough of this man. The vampire who had been involved with The League was not the one in the shower with her now. She somehow knew his soul and he had changed. They were truly soul mates.

"Nothing would make me happier," Lorenz said. Afton knew there was a 'but' coming. She felt let down before he even had a chance to explain why he was not going to have sex with her again. What could be more important than being together as one again? "Drake received word about who took you. He would not explain until after we made love and you were present."

Afton did not react to Drake commanding they make love, they were going to do it regardless. She had planned Lorenz's seduction down to the removal of the red lace dress, something she had rehearsed several times until she had it down.

What had grabbed her attention was that Drake had information regarding Malice. She knew things were not over in regards to that monster. This time she was going to fight him, with Lorenz right next to her.

"Do you feel any different?" she asked him. "Folklore mentioned, we would transform, but the stories were not specific about into what. It has to be more than just the ability to feed ourselves from sexual energy. We are going to need every advantage we can garnish against whomever Malice really is. Obviously he is more powerful than I had thought, since Drake is concerned."

"I would imagine it will come on slowly," Lorenz answered, "unlike your change after you first took my arterial blood. When I first was turned, my strength came on gradually. Each cell has to absorb the new blood and go through various cell divisions before we will truly know what we are now capable of."

"What about the telepathic channel?"

"It should have always existed, I just never tried to use it before." Lorenz admitted. "I fought joining with you from the start of the contract. My feelings changed as soon as I saw you, but I still had some issues I had to work through, before my soul was able to recognize what was before it. Alex's unborn child has already communicated to Drake."

Afton turned off the shower, the water was getting cold anyway. She exited the shower and wrapped a towel around her body. Thankfully Lorenz did the same thing. It was hard to concentrate with him standing naked in front of her. What would a couple of hours mean in the grand scheme of things if they were going to war against Malice?

Just thinking about Malice killed any sexual thoughts still lingering in her brain. Afton left the bathroom and went to the chest of drawers in which her new clothes were placed. She quickly dressed, as Lorenz did the same.

"Let's find out what Drake has discovered," Afton said. A saying flashed in her mind: revenge is a dish best served cold. She was ready to bring on the ice!

Chapter 17

⁓

Screams echoed through the passageway as she made her way with Lorenz to the main hall. Whoever was emitting those cries was in agony. They were cries she would not soon forget, they reflected more than physical pain. When they entered the room, she saw Drake feeding from an unfortunate man.

Afton recognized him immediately, Raine Narmouth. Although he was guilty of an unforgivable crime, she could not watch him being tortured. She knew firsthand how painful vampire venom was, if not accompanied by a numbing agent or the victim compelled to enjoy the experience. The man did not have on a stitch of clothing and vampire violence evident all over his body.

"I thought you required all blood donors be healed," Afton addressed Lorenz. He stood next to her watching the spectacle. Drake seemed to be taking unusual pleasure in the pain he was inflicting.

"Under normal circumstances, yes," Lorenz replied, not letting his eyes roam from the feeding before him. "This man does not fall under my protection. He is Drake's personal property." Afton could not believe those words came from the man she had just been intimate with.

She kept forgetting she was not dealing with human beings, but animalistic vampires. They were primarily ruled by their thirst for blood and obviously, revenge. In Drake's case, his victimization of Raine Narmouth went deeper.

If the child was in fact his soul mate, Drake was reacting to the oldest instinct known to any species: the protection of his mate. Regardless of Drake's motivations, the treatment of the man before her was excessive. Suddenly she felt dirty and had an overwhelming need to wash Lorenz's touch from her body. Afton knew he was capable of acting as Drake presently was.

Lorenz grabbed her arm, startling her. "Do not judge our relationship by what you see before you." Had he read her mind? "On second thought, feast your eyes on what is occurring. When I catch Malice and any vampire or human who assisted him, they will meet the same fate. I will drain them again and again, inflicting as much pain as I can. They will pay dearly for what they did to you. It will also be a warning to anyone or anything that considers harming what is mine."

Afton stood mute, not trusting anything that came out of her mouth. She'd be lying to herself if she did not get a perverse thrill from what Lorenz said. Had the joining started to rip away her humanity?

Drake released Raine Narmouth and wiped the remnants of blood from his mouth with the back of his hand. Several servants came forward and dragged Narmouth out of the room. Afton did not bother to ask what was going to happen to him. His wounds would be attended to, but not healed. He would also be given an injection to speed up blood production. All to prepare him for the next time Drake drained him. The condemned man knew this would continue until the child Alex carried took her first breath. At that point his suffering would end, with Drake finally taking the last drop of his blood.

It would be pointless to ask for mercy on Raine's behalf, even if she was so inclined. They left their quarters with the single mindedness to plan the capture and punishment of Malice for his crimes against Afton. She wanted him to pay for all the half-lings he had a hand in eliminating. If he was tortured as Raine Narmouth had, Afton doubted she would ask Drake or Lorenz to stop.

Disgusted with herself, Afton sat on a chair not far from a small pool of blood left behind from Raine. The scent almost made her sick to her stomach. It was the first time she had reacted thus to blood. She knew it had nothing to do with who the blood had come from, but what she had just experienced with Lorenz.

"End the suspense, Drake," Lorenz said. "Who is this Malice character?"

Afton shifted forward in her chair. She knew whatever Drake said would be meaningless to her. Her eyes were glued on Lorenz, so she could see his reaction to Drake's information.

"Wylaine," Drake uttered.

Lorenz just stared at Drake, his expression emotionless. Her soul mate's reaction momentarily confused Afton, but she felt anger building within him. How odd the joining had given her the ability to read his moods. The telepathic bond between them was expanding beyond just having the ability to communicate.

For what felt like an endless amount of time, Afton finally could not hold back asking any longer. "Who is Wylaine?"

Silence greeted her question, as it had since Drake mentioned who Malice really was. Looks were passed between Lorenz and Drake. Afton's patience was running thin, she wanted an answer. If she was able to read Lorenz's emotions, she assumed he could do the same. He had better answer her, and fast.

She was just about to get up and leave, when Lorenz finally found his voice. "Stay," was all he managed to say.

"I want to know who held me for seven days and violated me with his repulsive touch," Afton demanded.

"He is my brother," Lorenz confessed.

"So, he is one of your blood brothers," Afton responded. "Get the rest of your clan together and eliminate him." She was surprised by her reaction and the bloodthirsty tone in her voice.

"No, he is more than a blood brother. We shared the same birth parents."

Afton did not know how to react to Lorenz's revelation. The brothers shared the same genetic code passed on from their parents. Both brothers had been turned into vampires, although only Lorenz had maintained part of his humanity. Malice, or rather Wylaine, spoke so easily of his brother's demise.

"Does he want me because of you?" It was a twisted Cain and Able story. The ramifications of the brothers' relationship were unfathomable.

"Honestly, I have no idea." Lorenz ran his hands through his hair, appearing as affected by Drake's news as she was. "When we were human, we had a healthy sibling rivalry, pushing each other to succeed. He was turned before I was and came to me to offer me immortality. I saw what he became and declined his offer. In hindsight, I would have turned him down in kinder terms." Afton could see regret reflected in her soul mate's eyes, even after all this time.

"When were you finally turned?" Afton inquired.

"That was partially my doing," Drake admitted. "Wylaine was a particularly ruthless vampire. The Creator sent me to investigate his sibling to ascertain if there was a possibility we were going to have to deal with another like Wylaine. It was my duty to eliminate Lorenz if I felt he was a threat. When I met Lorenz, I knew he was different. He had a passion for life we look for when we select candidates to change. I went back to The Creator and asked for permission to turn Lorenz."

"You have to ask for permission to change someone into a vampire?" That surprised Afton, she thought it was a hit or miss sort of thing. She turned to her soul mate and said, "You took Drake up on his offer?"

"Not exactly," Lorenz answered.

"How exactly was it?" For the first time Afton considered the possibility that Lorenz had been changed against his will. She could not imagine the horror her soul mate must have endured.

"The Creator's blood is very powerful," Drake continued. "Any vampire within three generations of the original blood must get permission before he shares his gift. However, the Creator himself decided to turn Lorenz. He did this because the strength contained in his blood would give Lorenz a better chance against his brother."

"So you accepted The Creator's invitation to join them?" There was enough doubt in Afton's mind to pose the question, rather than taking it for granted. The look on her soul mate's face, made her doubt he willingly gave himself to The Creator.

"The chance of having a weapon against Wylaine was too much of a temptation. The Creator changed me without asking." The hopelessness of the man he once was, made Lorenz's delivery monotone. Afton could not imagine what the newly turned Lorenz had gone through, all to destroy a brother he had once loved. "Ironically, enough of my humanity was retained, making it impossible for me to harm my brother.

"For centuries I walked the tightrope between aligning myself with my blood brothers or my true brother. That is what originally brought me to The League. Wylaine was obsessed with their principles and I was searching for answers. It was a sick sense of loyalty that kept me with that group for so long. Over time, what I had once felt for my brother eroded, until only contempt remained. Your mother's kidnapping and planned fate were the severing point."

It was a tragic story and Afton had been placed before each of the brothers to be the latest pawn in their tug of war relationship. Where she was concerned, Wylaine's contempt toward half-lings had been trumped by his rivalry with Lorenz. He wanted to possess what had been contractually been given to his brother.

One thing was clear to Afton, Lorenz had been an unwilling participant in all of this. She shuffled the small distance that separated them and brought her lips to Lorenz's. The kiss started as a gentle sign of support, but turned into a means to restore each other's energy.

Energy soared through Lorenz's system as he devoured Afton's lips. No blood exchange had been this powerful, although it still paled in comparison to taking her blood or her body. The fact that he would never have to drink from another soul again, fueled his elated mood, as his body continued to take nourishment from her kiss.

He released her when he knew they had reached the saturation point. The last thing he wanted to do was cause Afton to experience blood seeping through her pores. She appeared dazed from the kiss. Momentarily, he feared he had taken her energy and left her weak.

"Wow, what a rush," Afton said as she fell back into the chair. Her complexion had a pink tint to it, showing she had been fed from the exchange as well.

"Obviously, the joining was successful," Drake said. "However, we need to get back to the problem at hand. I have sent for Frazour. Knowing him, he will drop everything and arrive before the sun rises."

Just his name caused shivers down Lorenz's spine. Of all his blood brothers, Frazour and he never seemed to connect on any level. They were polar opposites. Lorenz was the most human of all The Creator's clan, while Frazour did not appear he ever was anything other than a vampire. He reveled in the monster he was, although he never took it far enough to fall out of disfavor with The Creator. In fact, Frazour was the tool The Creator used when he wanted something done, when he did not have the stomach to do it himself.

Afton was chomping at the bit, desperate to know about Frazour. He glanced over at Drake, hoping he would provide the necessary information to his soul mate. Drake was well aware of the division that existed between the two vampires. Lorenz did not want his opinion of his other blood brother to prejudice Afton. He wanted her to be weary of Frazour, but not terrified of him. She had been through enough already.

"It would be best for you to stay in your rooms when Frazour arrives." It was clear Drake was addressing Afton. "Your father's men are blood-lusting because they have starved for so long, even what little blood they receive now has little impact on their eternal hunger. When Frazour was turned he had the strength of The Creator's blood, but never seemed to be able to manage his thirst. Right or wrong does not seem to be something he understands, your world would call him a psychopath."

Her once rosy cheeks paled before his eyes. "And we need him, why?" She must have realized the vampire threatened everything Lorenz had established here.

"What better way to stop a monster, then to send another after him," Drake reasoned. "Besides, the two have a history. When Lorenz's conversion did not reap the benefits he had hoped, The Creator went after someone he felt would not have any qualms doing what needed to be done. So a monster was created to stop another. Unfortunately, in their first altercation Wylaine prevailed. They have been playing a game of cat and mouse since. There are times Lorenz's brother will go into hiding and other times he is visible, just to taunt Frazour."

"Do you know what the definition of insanity is?" Afton asked. She did not give him or Drake a chance to reply before she gave them the answer. "It is doing the same thing over and over again, expecting a different outcome. Why is this time different from all the other attempts that have been made to bring down Wylaine?"

"You," both Drake and Lorenz answered at the same time.

"Wylaine has never seemed to care about anything," Drake said. "For some reason he has fixated on you. Not unlike the lunatic I just fed on, focused on Alexandra. His desire to possess you, to take you away from Lorenz, will lead to his downfall."

"You are going to use me as bait?" Afton asked incredulously. Lorenz could feel his soul mate's unease.

"Never," Lorenz tried to reassure her. "You do not have to be present to play a major factor in bringing down my brother. He is really quite brilliant, but he has become irrational where you are concerned. It was too easy to find you. We would have rescued you sooner, but we needed the Troyk crystal telepath's assistance. Our spies communicated you were physically all right. The small blood exchange was enough to safeguard you until we were able to execute our plans."

He knew what she had been through during her captivity. It was impossible for him to put his brother's treatment of his soul mate in words. Lorenz would spend the rest of Afton's life, making her forget those seven days. Fortunately, she did not push forward to discuss what she had suffered. Eventually they would talk about it, probably once they neutralized his brother.

"He will try again," Drake said, "but this time we will be ready. Frazour will arrive covertly. As far as Wylaine knows, there are only the three of us here with the servants. I will make a big production of leaving just prior to Wylaine arriving and double back."

"News of your transformation is already spreading," Lorenz continued. "Wylaine will not be able to stay away. He will find a means to enter this keep in order to recapture you. This time we will not be caught unaware of the risk he presents."

Afton did not look convinced. To be truthful, Lorenz's words reflected more confidence than he possessed. His main focus was to reassure his soul mate that she was safe. Lorenz would be the one who would have the sleepless nights and anxiety attacks until his brother finally made his move. He figured it would be sooner than later.

Chapter 18

Afton was dismissed from their presence, as if she was a small child being sent to her room. If she was thinking rationally, she would have reasoned that Lorenz and Drake had been fighting side by side for thousands of years. They probably knew what the other would do in battle before the other sprang into action. She was the wild card, the one they did not know or trust to have their back.

But she was not thinking straight. Adrenaline was coursing through her veins, courtesy of Lorenz's feral vampire side. Their joining had allowed her to share feelings with her soul mate. She was ill-equipped to deal with the instinctual urges consuming her.

If Malice presented himself to her now, Afton would want to tear him apart with her bare hands, even though she did not have the strength to support such a desire. Yet again, the transformation had been flawed, she thought as she ran her fingers through her knotted hair. Afton figured she was still in some transitional phase, as the joining continued to allow her to evolve.

When she arrived at her rooms, Afton dismissed the guards. She had exchanged one prison for another, although here she shared her quarters with Lorenz. Desire ran through her as she thought of her soul mate, only adding to her heightened state.

Too hyper to be caged, she went through the hidden door Lenore had showed her earlier, which led to a large courtyard. Bright purple light washed over her as she left the confines of the keep. The sun beating through the tarp was intense, but it felt great on what skin she had exposed.

Afton raised her face toward the tarp and soaked in the filtered light. Warmth bathed her skin and energized her body. She had not reacted to the sunlight in this fashion when she had spent time in her father's or Malice's courtyards. Something miraculous had happened to her body because of the joining.

Afton headed for the outer door, which led to the uncovered outdoors. Her earlier fears of the joining adversely impacting her ability to withstand the sun were all but forgotten. Afton left the stronghold's protection, determined to have some peace.

Energy soared through her system, as the sun beat down on her. It felt different than the power she gained from either blood or her new-found soul mate sexual exchange. Her vision seemed to be sharper, as if she had been looking through a dirty lens her whole life. She was able to see things in the distance that she knew normally she would not be able to ascertain.

The ultraviolet rays or whatever she had been reacting to also helped ground her. Suddenly she was able to manage all the emotions and urges that had been overwhelming her. The sun was providing her a different kind of energy. She did not know if it gave her just inner-strength or if she could generate some kind of power from what her pores soaked in. It was so much better than her skin excreting blood.

"Afton!" she heard Lenore call and she turned to converse with her friend. The shock on her servant's face concerned her.

"What is wrong?" Part of her did not want to know, Lenore's voice ripped her from experiencing everything the sun had done to her.

"Your skin," Lenore responded, "you have a beautiful tan."

Afton glanced at her arms, staring in disbelief at their bronze color. For someone who had shied away from her reflection most of her life, Afton had an overwhelming desire to look at her reflection. She ran past Lenore, through the courtyard, and ultimately back into her bedroom.

She stood before a full-length mirror and stared. The transformation had left her with a pearl-translucent complexion, now she glowed with a healthy tan. She could stand between Cassie and Darden in the California tourism advertisement, she thought about earlier when she met them on Earth.

Afton pulled back the neckline of the shirt she word to see if she had tan marks. She stared in wonder. Her exposure to the sun had changed the color of her skin, even where it had been sheltered by her clothing.

"It appears where exposure to filtered light drains a vampire's energy," Lenore reasoned, "the sun does the opposite with you. The discoloration of your skin must be a side-effect of the power you absorbed."

Afton got her fill of admiring herself in the mirror, she had always wanted a rich tan. She went to the chest of drawers, to test her physical strength. Being overly optimistic, she placed her index finger on the piece of furniture and pushed her digit forward.

Not surprisingly, the object did not move. Afton had not gotten super-human strength as of yet. This time she placed both palms on the side of the chest and pushed. To her amazement, it actually moved. Yesterday she would not have been able to manage what she accomplished with very little effort. Lorenz had warned her she would grow into her powers gradually.

"I am no longer sensitive to the sun, do not have to feed on humans, and have considerably more strength," Afton summarized. "Is there anything else I should test for?" She looked at Lenore with an expectant glance.

Her servant considered her question. "Give yourself a small cut and see how quickly you heal."

Brilliant! Afton reached for a small knife that sat on the top of the chest. It was the Nightshade equivalent of a Swiss Army knife. She made a small incision on the side of her forearm. The cut was shallow, but she quickly started to bleed. Right before her eyes, the skin mended itself. Afton took a tissue and wiped away the blood she had shed. She examined her arm and it showed no sign of the cut, not even a little scar.

"What does it mean?" Afton asked. Lenore had the look of someone who had just witnessed what she had expected to see. Afton was still blown-away by what had occurred.

"You have given your soul mate the sun and he has given you immortality."

Afton was not sure what she expected Lenore to say, but it certainly wasn't having anything to do with eternity. The concept of living forever was so new, she was not sure how she felt about it. She had never imagined that the transformation would have impacted her mortality.

She'd had snippets of happiness over the years, but overall her life had been depressing. Mortality had been a consoling thought, nothing could last forever. It was a sobering notion to think she could now be immortal.

"No one is invincible," Lenore said, as if she was reading Afton's thoughts. "Your body has the ability to heal itself; however, there can be some injuries that your body would not be able to fix. Keeping your head on your shoulders is a good start."

Indirectly Lenore was telling her decapitation would kill her, the thought was disturbing, but in an odd way reassuring. The thought of Marie Antoinette walking toward the guillotine raced through her mind. "This conversation has gotten too morbid. Let's go outside and explore."

Lorenz procrastinated returning to the rooms he now shared with Afton. He knew she was not happy about being excused when he and Drake started preliminary discussions about how to go about trapping Wylaine. Afton was too much of a distraction, even when she was gone from the room. They would finalize their strategy when Frazour arrived. His feral blood brother knew Wylaine better than any creature alive.

He greeted the men who stood outside his quarters and entered, immediately planning to see a dour Afton. He entered to find an empty room. Dread hit him hard, believing his brother had already recaptured his soul mate. He turned to talk to his men when he heard female laughter.

A door he had forgotten existed opened and two women stepped through the threshold. Once again, he did not immediately recognize Afton. Her skin was golden brown. How was that even possible? When she saw him, he was awarded with a beautiful smile. Afton's teeth appeared whiter due to her dark tan.

His soul mate launched herself into his arms. She was talking a mile a minute, as she dusted his face with light kisses. He had never seen this side of her personality before, happiness.

"You have to come with me to the courtyard and see how the filtered sunlight affects you," she managed to say between kisses. "I went past the tarp and the sun invigorated me for the first time in my life. We need to build a pool."

The last statement shocked Lorenz. Afton had finally lost her sanity after everything she had been through. They would soon be fighting for their lives and she wanted a swimming pool.

"Don't look at me like I'm crazy," Afton complained. "We need to see what the sun does to you, now that we have completed the joining. It could be built into our plan against Malice."

"Afton," Lorenz needed to herd Afton back to reality. "I cannot afford to be weakened by the sun right now. My brother can attack any minute."

"I know, that is why we need to see what effect the sun has on you. If your transformation was similar to mine, the sun should now give you energy, rather than draining you. Besides, if I am wrong, we will immediately return to the keep if you feel fatigue setting in."

It was true, he had never seen Afton like this before. He took her in his arms and brought his lips to hers. The power that was transferred from her was unlike anything that came before. Lorenz was still hesitant to follow her outside though. The weakness he had experienced after the train wreck was still heavy on his mind. He had been helpless as Afton was taken from him.

"Come on," Afton said encouragingly. She was literally dragging him to the passageway's door. "We need every advantage we can muster against Wylaine. I guarantee, he will not be rejuvenated by the sun."

The change in her was too pronounced to ignore. If the sun drained him as he expected, he merely had to make love to his soul mate to restore himself. She was overflowing with excess energy. It also made her sexy as hell. He nodded his consent and before he knew it, she was leading him toward the courtyard.

They reached the midway mark in the hallway where he normally began to feel the negative effects of the sun. It had been centuries since he had taken the passageway. This time he started to feel an emotional warmth spread through his body. It was not incendiary, but a different type of power he had not felt before. He quickened his pace, eager to reach the out of doors.

When they reached the outside, he had only one thing on his energy buzzed mind. He wanted to be inside his soul mate, as pagans long ago worshiped the sun. "Where did Lenore go off to?" he asked as he brought Afton down onto the grass. The last thing he wanted was to have her servant interrupt them.

"*She is seeing about a new female who escaped from another hive and has asked for sanctuary,*" Afton answered telepathically. Her mouth was now adhered to him, as they shared energy.

115

He made quick work of stripping the clothes from her body. She wore too many layers and he was going to have to do something about that in the future. Lorenz wanted quicker access to her body. It was doubtful his urgency for her was ever going to wane.

Lorenz entered her with one powerful thrust. He pitched back his head and screamed, reacting to a primal drive he was unable to explain. He entered and withdrew from her, as his hands explored her newly tanned body. Physically she had not changed since her initial transformation; however, there was a new vitality to her. Afton's new intensity fed him like never before. Her energy saturated his cells, as blood never did.

"Wrap your legs around my waist," Lorenz commanded. "I need to be deeper inside you." Afton complied almost immediately. He doubted he would ever be able to get deep enough or stay within her long enough to truly quench his thirst for her. When they finished dealing with Wylaine, he would find a spot in the Nightshade universe and spend the rest of his life catering to his soul mate and his unending desire for her.

Afton's breathing became labored as he hit the crest of a powerful orgasm. She did not have the strength of a vampire, but she managed to keep up with his frenzied pace. He pulled her into his arms after she finally collapsed her grasp on his torso.

"Wow," Afton managed to say. "We were able to manage that with diffused light. I cannot imagine what will happen when we have sex in the direct sunlight."

Lorenz was not sure what bothered him more, the idea of walking into full sunlight or Afton calling what they just experienced together sex. It was so much more than just releasing his physical need caused by his obsession to possess her body. Definitely more than the need to feed, he had already been sated from their last interchange. It was the coming together of soul mates.

"Afton, we are looking for Lorenz," a voice came from the entrance into his keep. "Drake is demanding his presence. Something has arrived."

It took little effort to decipher Frazour had arrived. People generally had issues describing his blood brother. 'Thing' came as close to an accurate description as he had heard.

"I know you do not want me in the same room with Frazour," Afton said. "But it's my life we are talking about and I want a seat at the table when we talk about bringing Malice down. Maybe it will stop some of the nightmares I have had since I was captured by your brother."

Lorenz wished he could turn down her request. He had a biological need to protect her. But he also knew she was no longer the sickly half-ling Yorik was able to terrorize and control. If she was part of the plan, Afton would gain the confidence to take her powers to the next level. She would not continue to evolve if he kept her locked in their bedroom, as much as he would like to do exactly that. Besides, it was next to impossible to deny her anything, as she lay naked below him.

"Fine," Lorenz conceded. "Do not look Frazour directly in the eyes. He is a powerful predator and you cannot present a challenge to him." Afton humphed a reply. She was not taking him seriously. "I am not speaking to hear my own voice. This is not a game. Frazour can teach your father a thing or two about brutality."

Lorenz could both see and feel the shudder escape from his soul mate. He wished he had been exaggerating the threat Frazour represented. If anything, he had downplayed the danger his blood brother was capable of producing.

Chapter 19

Lorenz's words played through her mind as Afton made her way to Lenore's quarters. Was Frazour the beast Lorenz had painted him to be? It was too late to back down now, besides, she had responsibilities to the community to also deal with. Afton wanted to check on the female refugee before she joined her soul mate and his two blood brothers. She heard weeping as she reached the door's threshold.

Lenore was on her knees trying to comfort the hysterical woman. The girl's face was hidden by her hands and red wavy hair. It was a head of hair Afton would have envied at one time. Now she knew the challenges wavy hair presented and understood why the girl kept it shoulder length. Moving past the ridiculous, shallow thought, Afton joined the two women. The girl was whimpering, mumbling incoherent words.

"What happened?" Afton questioned. The girl was safe, Afton could not understand why she was having a breakdown. It was then that she noticed the bruising on her arms. Were they fresh injuries or old wounds inflicted where she had been previously held?

"This is Emma," Lenore said, as she looked over her shoulder. "We were coming back from the great hall when she was attacked by a visiting vampire."

Frazour. Afton knew the newly arrived guest had been responsible for terrorizing the girl. She could sympathize what it would feel like to know you were safe one minute, only to be in peril the next.

"Did he feed on her? Was he responsible for the bruises?" Afton inquired.

"No, he did not feed on her," Lenore responded. "He grabbed her and declared she was now his. I do not know if she had the black and blue marks before she arrived. Drake interceded and freed Emma. I had never seen a vampire obsessed as he appeared to be with Emma." Lenore got up and motioned for Afton to join her in the far corner of the room. "There is something else you should know. The girl carries the gene. Drake mentioned it before I removed Emma. It may have been what set off the other vampire."

Wonderful! It was not necessary for Lenore to clarify which gene she was referring to. Now they not only had to deal with Frazour on Emma's behalf, but The League, as well. What she would not give to take a day off from the ruin of her life and spend the day on a Caribbean beach.

Afton returned to the girl, squatted, and gently grabbed her wrists. "You are safe now. I am sorry you were attacked in my home." It was odd referring to Lorenz's stronghold in those terms. "That animal will not approach you in that manner again. You have my word."

The girl lowered her hands and looked at her through the greenest eyes Afton had ever seen. "I just want to go home," Emma cried.

"Where is home?" If they could pinpoint where Emma was from, the next time Shirl returned, she could take Emma back to her own universe. For a moment Afton thought it would be nice to return to Earth and get her old boring life back. Now that she had Lorenz, she knew that would never happen.

"I live in San Diego, but I was hiking in Sedona when I somehow was transported here. There had been reports about two missing women, but I disregarded them. You never think it could happen to you. I was so stupid."

Afton smiled, she couldn't help it. "Today is your lucky day. I know a woman who can navigate the portal you fell through. Ironically, she was one of those missing women. As soon as she returns to the Nightshade universe, I will have her return you to Earth."

Emma looked at Afton in wonder. It was obvious she was too shocked to reply. Tears of relief fell down Emma's cheek as she nodded her understanding. The girl was beautiful, she could understand why Frazour had been attracted to her. It was obvious the she needed to be safeguarded against The League, as well as their visitor. Afton needed to speak to Lorenz about placing guards to protect Emma.

"I need to join Lorenz and his blood brothers," Afton said. "At least we can immediately deal with the vampire who assaulted Emma. Lorenz has certain rules of behavior, he expects from vampires who live in or visit his home. He will make sure the creature leaves Emma alone."

Afton left the two women and headed to the main chamber of Lorenz's keep. She was not looking forward to confronting Frazour and telling him Emma was off limits. Even after all of Lorenz's warnings, she was going to battle with the feral vampire.

She hoped the powers she gained during the transformation were now in place for her to use. If she had to confront Frazour with her limited strength, she knew she would be up a creek without a paddle. As a matter of fact, that situation seemed like a picnic compared to what she was about to face.

Afton stopped dead in her tracks when she got her first look at Frazour. Although The Creator's blood made him appear human, she could tell by looking at him he was something quite different. Everything about him cried predator, from the expression on his face, to the manner in which he stood.

He was clad all in black leather, which enhanced his short cut black hair. Blood-starved vampires outwardly represented the risk they presented, while with Frazour you could tell something was brewing under the surface. No wonder Emma was hysterical after being targeted by him. Every cell in her body cried for Afton to turn around and return to her bedroom. However, there was something that drew her forward. He was extremely handsome, in an ultra-bad-boy kind of way.

"Not now, Afton," Lorenz called as soon as he became aware of her presence. "Return to our quarters, I will join you there shortly."

In her mind Afton saw herself leaving the hall as quickly as her feet could move. Unfortunately, in reality, she was glued to the ground. Internally she struggled with removing herself from Frazour's presence, another part of her wanted to warn him to stay away from Emma. Self-preservation lost out as she moved forward.

"I just left a terrified woman." Afton did exactly what Lorenz had warned her not to do, she met Frazour's gaze in a direct challenge. "That girl is under my protection, and you will not approach her again in a threatening manner. If you cannot agree to that, then I want you to leave. We will deal with Lorenz's brother on our own."

Drake and her soul mate positioned themselves between Frazour and where she stood. She could feel a mixture of fear and pride coming from Lorenz. Afton knew she charted the right course, knowing Lorenz supported her.

Frazour approached her slowly, almost like a panther stalking its prey. She was mesmerized by the way he moved. There was an inherent sexiness to the man. Afton could almost see herself on her knees doing all sorts of unspeakable things to him.

"Release her," Lorenz growled.

Almost immediately whatever had possessed her was gone. Since arriving in the Nightshade universe, she had not been glamoured by a vampire. She could see how Shirl had fallen for Drake. It was a powerful weapon and Afton was grateful Lorenz had not used it against her.

"That was quite effective," Afton said. "Why did you not use it against Emma rather than terrorizing her?" She could not believe she was initiating this conversation with the animal in front of her, let alone giving him any ideas.

"Your mate shows courage, Lorenz," Frazour commented. His eyes roamed her body, making her feel uncomfortable. Only Lorenz had the right to look at her that way.

Lorenz turned and gave Afton a look of warning. A prudent person would back off at this point, but Afton seemed content digging her own grave. The best way to deal with Frazour was to gain his respect.

"Thank you for responding to Lorenz's summons," Afton continued. "He worked hard to create an environment where humans feel safe and willingly provide blood. I am sure you do not want to jeopardize all his hard work. There are many people who will be happy to give you nourishment. Arrangements have been made to provide you with whatever you require."

"And if I desire the girl I saw earlier?" Frazour asked.

"Well, then we have a problem," Afton answered. "Don't we?"

"We have lost focus on why Frazour is here," Drake broke into what had become a private battle between Afton and the feral vampire. "Let us focus on capturing Lorenz's brother. If you ask nicely, maybe the little girl who caught your eye earlier will participate in the celebration we have after the deed is done. Until then, all our focus needs to on bringing down Wylaine."

Although Drake had spoken, Frazour had not taken his gaze off Afton. She felt like he was still sizing her up and she needed to stick to her guns. They were involved in some perverted spitting contest and Afton was determined to win. With her gaze still locked on Frazour, Afton moved forward, moving past Lorenz and Drake. Her shield was gone and she was at the mercy of the predator before her.

"Will you talk to the girl on my behalf?" Frazour asked. The question surprised her. This feral animal generally took what he wanted. "I have no desire to feed off her. It appears my needs have been taken care of."

"Absolutely," Afton answered, "after we have accomplished our goal. In the meantime, leave her alone. She is obviously too much of a distraction. But if she does not desire to be with you, Frazour, you must respect her wishes."

His gaze was still focused on her, but Afton could see the beginning of a smile impact his lips. It was the first sign of vulnerability she had seen from Frazour. For the first time she could see the human side of this powerful vampire.

Lorenz came up from behind and gently grabbed her elbow. "Let us start planning to bring about Wylaine's demise, then we can talk about the girl's future."

"For as long as I have known your biological brother," Frazour said, "he has been obsessed with destroying anyone who threatens to pollute vampire blood, yet he believes he has a claim to your mate."

Afton was not going to continue to be referred to in that manner. "I have a name. You call me Afton and I will not call you all the names swimming through my mind right now."

The bud of a smile that had been evident on Frazour's face finally came into full bloom. His whole face transformed. This was a man she would actually consider going to bat for with Emma.

"Do not be misled in lowering your guard against my blood brother," Lorenz communicated telepathically. *"His charm is just a smoke screen to disguise what he is capable of destroying. He is the most lethal creature I have ever come across in my life."*

Afton did not react to Lorenz's warning. She could put up a front as well as the one Frazour presented. After all, she had managed to survive in her father's hive for just over a month and seven days with Malice.

"So, I am going to be bait," she announced loudly.

Chapter 20

They convened in the main hall, humans and vampires banding together. It was the quiet before the storm. No one knew when Malice would attack, but the goosebumps evident on her skin told her it would be soon. She was not the only one in danger, the lifestyle Lorenz had managed to nurture for all who lived within these walls was at risk. On top of everything else, they now had a woman residing among them who carried the genetic marker. There was so much to lose if they were not victorious.

Drake had just returned. She understood he made quite a spectacle of himself at Yorik's hive, retiring with three women. Anyone who knew of Drake's reputation would not expect him to reemerge for a minimum of two days. Hopefully, Malice's spies who might be residing in her father's hive, would communicate Drake's actions.

Shifting her gaze from Drake, Afton's eyes fell on Frazour. He was staring intently at Emma, who sat beside Lenore at the end of the table. The guards Lorenz had assigned to watch over Emma were directly behind her. Although she did not like the way he was looking at the woman, Afton knew it was pointless to command him not to look at the beautiful redhead. Her unease for Emma's safety was compounded by the dread she felt waiting for Malice's attack.

This was not the calm before the storm after all, she was in the eye of a hurricane. Any direction she turned in this world was fraught with danger. Even after they dealt with Malice, there was still The League and the threat they posed. She and Emma would never find peace in the Nightshade universe.

Shirl would portal Emma to Earth, but Afton would never return to her old life. She was forever tied to Lorenz. Whatever they ended up evolving into, their destinies were now one and the same. It was doubtful they belonged in either world, there was no safe haven waiting for them at the end of this battle.

"Frazour is going to show you some defensive moves you can use when the attack starts," Lorenz said as he leaned into her. Warmth radiated off his body, relieving the chill, her thoughts had brought on. This man had become the light of her life, lifting her from the darkness.

"If my body has not developed any more muscle mass, I don't know what good it will do," Afton confessed. A shiver ran through her body as Lorenz brushed his fingers across her bicep.

"A vampire's strength comes from his blood." Lorenz continued to caress her upper arm, slowly driving her mad. "You need to draw on the power of the blood we shared. The Creator's life-force which courses through your veins can overpower almost any vampire that comes at you."

"Except for Malice," Afton figured she would finish Lorenz's sentence. She did not stand a chance against the vampire who wanted to possess her.

"To be honest," Lorenz continued, "I do not know. Some vampires who are made are incredibly powerful, even without The Creator's blood. Almost from the beginning, Wylaine was a force to be reckoned with. One of the three of us will be with you at all times and we will deal with my brother."

Afton still could not bring herself to call Malice by his given name. It would make her view him as once being human, a brother who loved his sibling. In her eyes, she needed to view him as the monster he had become, one who wanted to harm her and kill her soul mate.

Although she trusted Drake more than Lorenz's other blood brother, Afton knew she needed to continue to protect Emma. "When we are not together, I want Frazour by my side. The Creator made him purposely to deal with your true brother. There must have been a reason why he was chosen, so I will feel better with him when I cannot have you near." As if a second thought came to her, Afton continued, "Drake should be plastered to Emma's side. She is in as much danger if any of Malice's brethren fight alongside him."

A brilliant smile emerged from Lorenz's face. It reflected she was not fooling him. It was odd seeing a vampire smile. She could not remember if he had smiled prior to the transformation. Drake would grin as part of his seductive routine, she doubted it was done out of joy.

Afton quickly corrected herself. When Drake was with Alex and her unborn child, he seemed almost giddy. For the first time, she seriously considered the baby could be Drake's soul mate. Should she continue to try to keep the two of them apart? She knew she would stop anyone who tried to separate her from Lorenz. The idea of ever losing him was more than she could bear.

"Since we are going to do battle shortly," Afton whispered in Lorenz's ear, "perhaps we should restore our energy." She shifted her head slightly and took his earlobe into her mouth. As she sucked on the tender morsel, she was rewarded with a guttural groan that came from Lorenz.

She was going to treasure every moment she had with this man, as if it were their last.

꒰ා

Afton was going to be the death of him yet, Lorenz thought as his soul mate made love to his ear. He should be thinking about battle strategies, instead of driving into her core. Unable to take any more he grabbed her arm, lifting her from where she had been seated.

He literally dragged her from the hall, not caring what the others thought. His urgency was too great to make it all the way to their quarters. Lorenz led her down an isolated hallway and opened the first door they came to. The room was used for storage, not the most comfortable place to make love to Afton.

Lorenz lifted her into his arms and brought her to stand between two cabinets. Without having to say a word, Afton wrapped her arms around his neck and her legs captured his waist. He fumbled to release himself from his pants, having lost control of anything but his need for her.

He grabbed the soft material of her dress and pulled it up to bunch around her waist. To his relief, she had followed his request not to wear undergarments. His fingers explored the junction between her legs, finding her wet and ready for him.

With the impatience of the teenager he had once been, he entered the woman in his arms. She had become his life, as necessary to him as breathing. He clasped his mouth to hers and captured the first of her moans. His urgency had eliminated all foreplay; in the past, he had spent more time preparing her for his invasion.

She snickered against his lips, as those thoughts must have penetrated the bond that now existed between the two of them. *"I surrender,"* she advised him telepathically, *"there is no need to discuss terms, just keep doing what you started."*

She rode him, having the ride of her life. Energy was exchanged, power that reinforced the bond between them. Somehow he knew the additional paranormal forces which germinated during the transformation ritual would continue to grow as they made love. This was what they were meant to do, not sitting in some stuffy room waiting to be attacked.

A primal cry escaped him seconds after he released her mouth. She pounded his shoulders with her fists, he knew without being told she had not reached her own release and he had better not stop now. His soul mate did not need a soft bed, all she needed was him. She was so tight he could barely stand it. All he had to do was hold on just a little longer and his mate would reach her climax.

Afton cried out as Lorenz released his seed into her womb. For the first time since his conversion, he knew he ejaculated life into a woman. He held her as he slowly recovered physically and mentally. Although Afton was once a half-ling, he never sensed the genetic marker in her. It really did not matter, since he was no longer a vampire and she was now the same creature he had become. What they had evolved into was beyond his understanding. He just knew they would continue their voyage together, two halves that made a whole.

He placed his forehead against hers. Just for an additional moment he wanted to enjoy the peace that momentarily came over him. It would not be long before he had to face his brother and temporarily release the love of his life. His feelings for her only reinforced he had to stop Wylaine once and for all.

His bliss was short lived as cries echoed through his stronghold.

Chapter 21

They quickly adjusted their clothing and Lorenz opened the cabinet closest to the door. It contained various weapons they had placed in storage, since the treaty not only protected them from Yorik's troops, but offered them protection against invasions from others. Until that moment, Lorenz had not considered Afton's father could have been called upon to provide assistance in their war against Wylaine.

Lorenz gazed at his soul mate, considering which weapons would be best to arm her with. He grabbed several sickles and daggers strategically placed in the weapon locker. In addition, he snagged a belt and placed it around Afton's waist.

"I do not imagine it would be acceptable for me to lock you in here while I take care of my brother?" Lorenz asked, knowing the answer before he saw it reflected in her face. "No, I did not think so. It was worth a try anyway."

"Just tell me what to do," Afton said, her voice laced with urgency. She was presenting a brave front, but he imagined she was terrified.

"Do not think, but react," Lorenz answered. "Your power will come from within. The transformation has made you a weapon, although you probably do not feel any different. Let the energy soar through your body and guide your arms and legs in battle. If you think about what you are doing, your mind may stop the instinctual actions and open you to danger. Follow the feelings that will overtake you and you will be fine."

Lorenz saw she was considering everything he had told her. Afton examined the sickle in her hand. She shifted her wrist, placing the weapon in motion.

The sickle moved smoothly through the air, Afton appeared to be a natural branding such a weapon.

"Beheading a vampire is the quickest way to dispatch an enemy," Lorenz informed her. "Swing for the head, the weapon will become an extension of you. Complete your follow through and move to the next vampire. Again, Afton, do not think. Pretend it is a game and you want to score as many points as possible."

"But it is not a game," his soul mate countered.

"No, it is not. But you cannot be weighed down by what you are about to do. These are soulless husks who serve no function other than to kill whomever they come across. They traded their humanity for the gift of immortality. My love, you are going to deprive them of their gift this day."

He could tell she was taken aback by the name he had just called her. It was a funny time to call her by an endearment for the first time. Lorenz had guarded his words, as he fought to contain the feelings that had been growing from within where his soul mate was concerned. They had everything to lose today. If they came out victorious, he would not only show her how he felt, but tell her as well.

"I placed two more sickles on your belt, just in case any of them get stuck in one of your victims. The daggers are for when you have no more sickles. With the knife, you have to get closer to your opponent. Their heart needs to be pierced. If you miss the first time, jab him again until he starts to disintegrate."

"Oh, God," Afton cried, "this is real." Lorenz could almost taste her fear.

"It does not have to be," Lorenz answered. "Pretend you are dreaming and nothing can harm you. Your transformation has made you invincible." He brought her into his arms and kissed her one last time. "We need to aid our friends and neighbors. Stay by my side as long as you can. Once you have started to fight the enemy, forget about me entirely. Just keep fighting until there is no longer a danger."

Afton nodded and returned his kiss. "When this is over, we are going to spend a week in bed." He could not help but smile at those words. "What? We need to restore our energy after everything we are about to do."

He loved this woman. If only he had told her before now, but it was not the right time to share his feelings with her. They needed to engage the enemy and he needed her to focus only on that. With no further words spoken, he opened the door and ran beside Afton to the center hall.

They encountered their first set of vampires, not far from the storage room. Afton tightened her grip around the sickle; she was ready to face their enemy. She concentrated on the power contained in her body, turning off her mind to the best of her ability. Energy coursed through her arms as she raised and swiped the weapon against the neck of the vampire who stood before her. As Lorenz instructed, she moved on, not giving the beheaded opponent a second thought.

Her soul mate was in front of her, making a path scattered with dead enemies in his wake. Afton finished off what he left behind. The floor was slick with blood, but her feet navigated through the sticky mess without sliding. When they entered the main hall Afton hesitated for a moment and took in all that was before her.

Their vampire allies were taking on the opponents, protecting the humans they co-existed with. Emma was among them, holding on to a dagger with all her might. She could see the strain in the woman's hands as Emma tightened her grip. Frazour fought not far from the girl. Obviously, he was protecting Emma, as Lorenz would have wished to protect her. Afton decided she would help to protect the humans rather than playing offense.

As she made her way to the humans, she had to navigate around those doing battle. Afton ascertained she could assist one of her allies and dispatched an enemy with her sickle. He went down quickly, the weapon still firmly in her grasp. The strength with which she was able to swing the weapon astounded her. Afton felt like an Amazon warrior of legend.

Out of nowhere a larger than usual vampire tackled her, momentarily knocking the wind out of her. Her instinct was to go for the knife in her belt rather than fighting to keep his fangs out of her neck. She knew she was not going to win the battle of time and needed to brace herself for his venomous bite.

Pain coursed through her body as he tore into her jugular. Afton concentrated on the power within her, rather than the liquid taken from her body. She reached for one of the daggers Lorenz had secured to her belt, but came up short in grabbing one of the weapons. The vampire on top of her shifted as he continued to gorge on her blood.

That simple movement cleared her way to clasp her hand around the dagger's hilt. She pulled it from its sheath and stabbed the vampire where she figured his heart was. Not feeling sure of making the mark, she continued thrusting the blade into his back until she was bathed in his dust. Afton had dispatched the vampire who thought he could bring her down.

She slowly got to her feet. Blood ran down her neck from the unhealed wound. Afton figured her body's ability to heal itself would make short work of the ripped flesh. There were humans she needed to protect, she did not have the luxury of worrying about the gash. Her focus was on saving the humans now under attack. Involuntarily, her hand went to her neck. Heat generated from the site of the attack. Her body was already healing itself.

Having lost the sickle and one of her daggers during the last attack, Afton reached into her belt and secured one more of each of the weapons. She felt like a super hero! Power continued to course through her, not impacted by the minor skirmish she had just come back victorious from. It was all a game she told herself and it was time to do more damage to the enemy.

Putting her injury aside, Afton continued toward the terrified group of humans. A small contingent of friendly vampires attempted to protect them. It appeared they were losing their battle. From her vantage point, it appeared two vampires were already feasting on two of the fallen humans.

Determined to protect them, Afton's body moved with incredible speed to help ward off the hostile creatures. She had witnessed her father's amazing pace when he attacked, but never thought she would have the ability. With her second sickle drawn, she brought down one of the vampires who was just about to attack one of the humans.

"Get behind me," she yelled. Although the woman she just saved barely knew her, certainly not enough to place her life in Afton's hands, she complied without thought. The loyal vampires, not fending off the enemy, positioned themselves around the remaining humans and Afton.

More vampires came at them than originally were attacking the humans. It was then that Afton realized she was placing them in greater danger. Malice had probably requested she be taken alive. Having no other choice, Afton pulled out her third sickle and moved away from the people she had originally come to protect.

Every vampire she had attracted followed as she made her way to the center of the battle. She hoped as Lorenz and his people finished off their prey, they would take on the vampires who followed her. There were too many of them to take on alone. Once again, Lorenz's words to react, not to think, played in her head. She lifted her weapons and attacked with every ounce of strength she had left.

She felt a sting of pain and looked down to see a blade embedded in her upper thigh. Almost simultaneously, she rammed one of her sickles into her opponent's side, pulled the dagger out of her leg, and rammed it into the vampire's chest. Both of her weapons fell to the ground as her opponent turned into a pile of dust. All those hours of watching *Buffy, The Vampire Slayer* now seemed like war preparation. She tried to emulate all of Sarah Michelle Gellar's moves.

Fatigue started to wear on her. Afton was not sure how much longer she was going to be able to keep up the pace she set. If she moved any slower, it was doubtful she would stand a chance against Malice's army. It was taking too much energy to both fight at the frequency she was and heal the wounds inflicted. One thing was clear, she was not going to allow herself to fall into Malice's hands again. She would sooner ram one of her blades into her own chest.

The vampire before her was putting up an excellent fight. She did not know if it was because she had lost her edge, he was a superior fighter, or a combination of both. All her attention was focused on her opponent, she was unaware of the attack on her flank until it was too late. Afton came down hard on her knees and felt excruciating pain, as a vampire who attacked from the rear sunk his fangs into her shoulder. More pain was generated from her arm and leg as her enemy swarmed around her fallen body.

Unable to stand the pain, Afton screamed. The creatures feeding off her seemed to get excited by the harm they were inflicting and her inability to withstand it. With no other choice, she reached out to Lorenz. She did not know how, but she was able to link in what she felt was a telepathic SOS. She no longer had the strength to communicate thoughts through their channel. As she continued to pulse out a cry for help, Afton could feel herself slip away.

Lorenz could see they were outnumbered and outclassed. Starving vampires fought with a frenzy his own forces could not match. He had caught sight of Drake and Frazour throughout the battle, they were holding their own against the enemy. There were just too many of them for his blood brothers to make an impact. At no point had he seen Wylaine. His brother was probably staying in the shadows until his forces had won.

Despite his desire to, Lorenz did not attempt to seek out Afton. He knew if he focused on her, whatever advantage he had against his enemy would be lost. If she was in mortal danger he would know and at that point come to her aid. The longer he fought without hearing from Afton, the more he was able to concentrate on the enemy before him.

Another vampire fell at his feet. Several of the enemy forces he brought down were juicier than he had expected, Lorenz was covered with arterial blood spray. He imagined just prior to the battle his opponents gorged to provide instant strength, although it would not feed their cells for any length of time.

A sudden pain brought him to his knees. He knew without checking his own body, the agony he felt was coming from Afton. He had to find her and quickly. Lorenz grabbed the weapons at his feet and got up to make his way to his soul mate.

He found her on the far side of the chamber with six vampires feeding on her. The half-ling's enriched blood had made her attackers sluggish, unprepared for his attack. He had dispatched four of them when a fresh set of enemy reinforcements descended on him. Lorenz could feel her life-force, weakening as he continued a losing battle to free them both.

For the first time, Lorenz internalized, they were going to lose this battle. By some miracle they had found each other, only to have fate rip them apart in such a violent manner. To make matters worse, he had not told her how he felt. When she called what they did sex, he should have corrected her right then and there. As far as she knew, he was using her to transcend.

"I love you, Afton," he communicated through their channel. Lorenz was disheartened when there was no response from her at his declaration. He wanted her to have the strength to hear him and know she was not going to die alone. With what little strength he had, Lorenz crawled and positioned himself over her body. He pulled out his dagger, making sure Wylaine was not going to victimize his soul mate ever again.

A cry penetrated his ears, stilling the hand that held the blade. He knew that sound, he just could not recall where he had heard it before. The noise in the room intensified, as metal met metal. It was then he knew friendly forces had come to support their efforts.

Energy flooded his body, generated by his newly found hope. He took the blade in his hand and thrust it into the vampire on his right, the one that posed the greatest threat to Afton. Lorenz rolled off his soul mate and threw two more daggers into the chests of the next two closest enemies. The remaining vampires fled, realizing the new army was overpowering the room.

Lorenz was now free to bring Afton into his arms. He was not sure if he had enough power to feed his weakened soul mate. She was covered in blood and had lost the tan she had previously possessed. Her sun-kissed skin must have paled as she burned the solar energy temporarily provided.

"All I asked of you was to take care of my daughter, and you could not even do that." Lorenz now knew it had been Yorik who had saved the day.

Lorenz rose, taking Afton with him. He cradled her head against his chest, hoping proximity would start the energy flowing between the two of them. Slightly shifting her in his arms, he brought his lips to hers. There was still no sign of life from Afton, other than a weak heartbeat.

Yorik walked to his side and brushed the hair out of Afton's face after Lorenz finished kissing her. "I heard stories, talked to Drake, yet still I have a hard time believing my eyes. My daughter transformed beyond my expectations."

There was a gentleness Lorenz had never seen Yorik exhibit toward his daughter. He had come to their aid without being asked and saved his daughter's life. Lorenz had failed to protect the light of his life.

"Take her to your quarters," Yorik commanded. "We will deal with the survivors and find Wylaine."

Lorenz nodded. "Whatever blood is reaped, belongs to you."

An odd sound, he assumed was laughter, came out of Yorik. "I was not considering anything else. Now, care for my daughter and we will talk more."

He left the great hall and carried Afton to their bedroom. All along the way he kept looking for signs that Afton was healing, but nothing was visible. Had her father been too late to save his soul mate?

Chapter 22

∿

She was running through a meadow of wild flowers, color exploding all around her. A lovely white halter dress covered her body, bringing out her beautiful alabaster shoulders. Her long black hair was flowing behind her, not a snag in sight. Under the shelter of a large oak tree Lorenz was there with a large picnic lunch, spread out on a blanket. Afton fell into Lorenz's arms and he kissed her with all the pent up passion her absence dictated.

Someone was shoving her, as her beautiful surroundings became cloudy, thick with fog. Regretfully, Afton knew she was transitioning from a wonderful dream back into the horrible reality of her life. She hesitated opening her eyes, wanting to prolong the dream a little longer. It was hopeless, she had lost her grip on the tranquil vision. Defeated, slowly she opened her eyes.

Lenore was beside her, still working to wake her from slumber. Why would her friend violate the sanctity of what little peace she had in this world? Where was her soul mate? Why wasn't he languishing next to her bed, shattered until she woke?

"Time to rise," Lenore informed her. "Lorenz and your father have suffered enough waiting for you to come back to consciousness. We need to dress you and allow everyone to see that you have recovered."

She had to still be dreaming, "My father?"

"Surprised everyone, your father did," Lenore said enthusiastically. "Here I always thought he was a monster, yet he saved the day." Afton could still see Yorik holding a blade to Lenore's neck, forcing Afton to drink the blood that flowed from the shallow cut he was responsible for making.

Images started to assault her when she digested all Lenore had to say. "The battle, how did things go?" She had thought all was lost. The feelings she had at losing Lorenz flooded her mind. Afton rose before Lenore could answer the question. Her servant's presence and what little information she shared indicated they won the day. The only question was how many casualties they suffered.

Afton stood by the bureau debating what to wear. She had come back from the dead and wanted to look her best. "I would wear the deep blue dress if I were you," Lenore recommended. It was a good choice, the color favored her light colored skin and her black hair. The golden tan had faded from her skin, no doubt because she expended all her energy. She ran her hand through her tresses and was stopped midway by a nest of snags. Attuned to Afton's reaction to her hair, Lenore continued, "We will deal with your hair later. Let me pin it up, we should immediately join Lorenz and the others."

She could not agree more. Afton wanted to know how things faired and whether they had captured Malice. She hoped they had already dispatched him, so she would not have to be involved in the decision concerning what to do about the monster.

Lenore made quick work of dealing with her hair and they were on their way to the great hall. When they arrived her father was at the table with Lorenz, Drake, and Frazour. Emma alone sat meekly at a nearby table. She hoped it was for the girl's protection and nothing nefarious planned by Frazour. Even after the battle, Afton still did not fully trust that particular blood brother.

As soon as Lorenz spotted Afton entering the room, he rose and greeted her with a kiss. Energy soared through her, as it did every time he kissed her. "Finally awake, I see," he said. She could not read what type of mood he was in. "I was worried sick when you did not awaken immediately after I passed part of my life-force to you."

"Let me see my girl," Yorik commanded. Afton had a short debate whether she should ignore her father. Considering he had saved all their lives, she decided to honor his request.

Afton presented herself before her father. His eyes devoured her, disbelief evident in his stare. "Now that I see you awake, it is even more unbelievable what you have transitioned into. For as long as stories about what became of The Creator circulated, I still did not believe in the fairy tale. You are both proof that portions are true. Do you still need to drink blood?"

"Neither of us do," Lorenz answered her father. "Although I have not entered direct sunlight, my proximity to it no longer weakens me. Afton can heal, although the battle took too much out of her at once."

Her father digested all that was provided. He appeared to be going over some type of mental checklist in his head. "What about compulsion? Do you have that gift?"

Once again, she was disappointed in her father's reaction. He continued to treat her like some type of experiment, but he did make a good point. Afton had not considered she would be able to use compulsion. She had not seen it in practice, so it was not in the forefront of her mind. Besides, everyone here did everything she asked, so it did not cross her mind to even try to use that particular power.

"I am not sure," Afton finally answered her father. "How does a vampire compel someone, and does it work on vampires?"

"Have you communicated telepathically to Lorenz?" Yorik asked.

Afton nodded, her mind taking the next logical steps in how compulsion would work. Once she knew how, the only question was who she would compel and to do what. Actually, this could be fun, if she picked the right subject.

"You project your thoughts to your mate, compulsion works the same way. The only difference is you need to have eye contact with whom you wish to compel. It is a skill you should practice, but against vampires. You have no need to compel humans." Her father was right. Had she been able to compel vampires during the battle, it would have been a handy trick.

"Does it only work on one vampire at a time?" Afton inquired.

"Naturally," her father answered. "Properly used, you would prevail in any one-on-one interchange.

Afton looked in Emma's direction and figured out she would try it against Frazour as soon as she had the opportunity. If she could compel Frazour to leave Emma alone, that would be one less thing for her to worry about. However, she wanted to make sure she mastered the gift before she dared use it against that particular vampire.

"Are there any instances where compulsion does not work, assuming I developed the gift?" She thought it was best to understand the power before she started to try her hand at it.

"A mind can be manipulated to do just about anything. However, if someone is dead set against something, there is nothing you can do. That includes mind control. I can compel you to drink the blood of your enemy, but I could not force you to harm your handmaiden."

Afton considered her father's words. If Yorik had compelled her once she entered the Nightshade universe, things would have been so much easier on her. She also considered her early relationship with Lorenz. She would not have been upset with her father had he compelled her, but it would have been a different story where Lorenz was concerned. She wanted to be sure the feelings she had for Lorenz were truly hers, not manufactured to advance someone's agenda related to her.

The conversation stalled and for the first time since entering the room, Afton wondered what happened to Malice. No one had brought up the subject of Lorenz's brother. She crossed her fingers as she asked the question of her soul mate.

"What did you end up doing with your brother?"

"After the battle, we searched the stronghold, but could not find him," Lorenz supplied. "We are not all together sure he was even present. When the train was attacked, he had used one of his henchmen, not risking being involved in an aborted attack."

Afton stumbled into the chair she had been standing next to. She had thought the danger was over, she was wrong. Was this nightmare ever going to end?

"What is being done to find and destroy him?" Afton was at the end of her rope, she did not care how bloodthirsty she sounded. Malice's desire for her had resulted in the deaths of countless humans and vampires who fought bravely beside her. Everyone was still in danger as long as Malice drew breath.

"I have my scouts out," Drake entered the conversation. "It will not be long before we discover where he is hiding and go on the offensive this time."

There was nothing more she could do on that front. "What of the human survivors? Are they being taken care of properly?"

"You know the type of community I run, Afton," Lorenz said with an edge to his voice. "Of course they are being cared for. This morning we buried the ten who died yesterday. We honored them for what they contributed to our home and we will mourn their passing."

Afton wished she could take back the stupid question and remove the look of hurt from her soul mate's face. Her mind had been consumed with thoughts of Malice, she had not properly considered her question before asking it. She had a single focus, until that monster was found and dealt with.

Lorenz could see Afton's complexion pale. She had been through so much this day, and yet she was still in danger from Wylaine. When he thought he had lost her, he was shattered. He gave her every ounce of energy he had until Drake pulled him away from his soul mate. To make matters worse, he once again owed Yorik a debt. He imagined the master vampire would not return to his hive until Afton was no longer in danger. Everyone in his home was on edge and Yorik's physical presence was not helping matters.

"I would like to see the graves of those who died in battle today," Afton whispered. "All of this is my fault. They would still be alive if I had not come here."

A choir of responses reacted to Afton's words, however he could tell his were the ones she most needed to hear. He got on his knees before her. "You are my soul mate, Afton," he started. "I care for you more than I do my own well-being. Fate brought us together. My brother is a lunatic and I started things in motion when I rescued your mother.

"What happened today was not your fault. You did nothing to provoke Wylaine, other than capture my heart." It was not the confession of love he wanted to give her, but it would do considering the audience around them. "When this is all over we will go in the daylight together and visit their final resting place, I promise."

The makings of a smile crossed Afton's face, but her eyes shone. He needed to get her alone and release all the anxiety pent up in his body since the battle. His hands were still coated with her dried blood. He had sworn he would not wash them until he knew she was well.

Warm hands were placed over his. He did not know if she was showing affection or if she sensed he still had her blood on the flesh she held. Heat continued to be generated, feeding him with energy and a feeling of contentment. How her touch soothed his soul.

"Is it a waiting game now, or is there anything we can do to prepare for our next battle with Malice?" Afton asked.

"Until we hear from my spies," Drake answered, "we wait. Why do you not try to compel me? If you have the power, I doubt it would work on Lorenz. There are other things you can use where he is concerned."

A smile blossomed on his soul mate's face. He knew she needed to be distracted and was more grateful, rather than jealous, that Drake had given her something to concentrate on. If she did have the power, it was also an excellent idea for her to start practicing using the gift to her advantage.

Lorenz loved watching Afton's facial expressions changing as she toyed with what she would compel Drake to do. She had an adorable way of crinkling her nose when she appeared to be discounting an idea. He would have loved to hear what was going on in that mind of hers, that orchestrated the looks reflected on her face, but nothing was leaking through their telepathic channel.

In all the time they had spent together, he was not sure he ever saw that particular nuance reflected on her lovely face. It was invigorating to know he was going to discover all sorts of things about his soul mate. They had an eternity together.

Afton leaned forward in her chair and stared across the table at Drake. A thousand likely scenarios raced through Lorenz's mind related to what she was going to have Drake perform. He immediately ruled out anything sexually related. His blood brother was the ultimate ladies' man and did not have to be pushed in that area.

"Drink from Yorik." That particular command had not been one of the items Lorenz had come up with. It was actually a brilliant test of her ability to compel.

Lorenz watched in disbelief as Drake rose and started toward the master vampire. He was curious what Yorik would do once Drake reached him. In a flash of movement, Drake went after Yorik's jugular and Yorik just as quickly had Drake on his back, a blade to his neck.

Afton catapulted to her feet and ran to where her father had Drake pinned to the ground. "Stop," Afton cried, desperately trying to make eye contact with Drake.

"Get off me," Drake yelled. "What in the name of The Creator is going on here?"

Sensing the danger was over, Yorik got back on his feet. In an unusual gesture, he offered his hand to Drake, assisting him up. "My daughter just compelled you to take my blood." If Lorenz was not mistaken, it sounded like Yorik was proud of Afton. "That was unexpected, little girl, but an excellent choice in testing your ability. Under normal circumstances, Drake would never have attempted such a disrespectful move."

Drake looked at Afton in wonder. "If you can compel someone as powerful as me in your first attempt, your gift is unparalleled."

Lorenz could not agree more, but he needed to make sure they were looking at this with the right perspective. "She can compel one vampire at a time, and only if she can stare him in the eye. Let us not declare victory just yet. I still want Frazour to train her in hand-to-hand combat. The least energy she uses fighting, the longer she will last."

"Let us do it now," Frazour responded. "I am tired of sitting around waiting for news. The first thing we need to do is get you out of that dress." Lorenz knew what his blood brother meant and took no offense to his words. However, it did not stop Lorenz from wanting to do exactly that with his soul mate. "Your legs need to be free to move in battle, plus you need armor. All the women should be properly suited regardless of their station."

He watched Frazour glance at Emma. There was a real attraction there, although it appeared to be one-sided. Lorenz noted Afton glancing between Frazour and Emma, frowning.

"To the armory then," Lorenz announced while he took Afton's hand.

As they walked side by side, he could not help but imagine his soul mate in a tight leather outfit, allowing her the freedom to fight. However, when he visualized her thus, he was there too, taking off her new outer layer, allowing him to enjoy her naked flesh. This war with Wylaine had to end, so Lorenz would properly enjoy his soul mate without any interruptions.

Chapter 23

~

Afton peeled off the makeshift cat suit she had worn while she sparred with Frazour. It clung to her like a second skin. She had never moved so fast or felt so alive, as she did when she fought. Well, there was one exception. She gingerly lifted the material from her shoulders, trying to miss the bruises. Although she healed quickly, bruising was another story. Her full-length mirror gave her a view of her black and blue body.

"I am going to kill Frazour," Lorenz said as he walked into their chamber and saw the damage that had been inflicted during their weapons training.

She turned to face her soul mate, in the process the leather-like material dug into one of her bruises. "Ouch!" Afton needed to get the damned costume off before she inflicted anymore unwanted pain on her poor body. It was not long before she was standing naked, only wearing boots.

"Let me help you with those," Lorenz said as he took her in his arms and walked toward the bed. He gently placed her on the mattress, careful not to further aggravate her wounded body. He unlaced the boots and pulled them off her feet. She was now totally exposed to him, her legs spread apart, just as he had left them. With a lecherous smile on his face, Lorenz pulled off his clothes in record time.

He grabbed her ankles and lifted them over his shoulders. She was pulled slowly toward him, his eyes never breaking contact with hers. When he had her exactly where he wanted her positioned, he brought his chest against the mattress and his head in proximity to her sex. She swallowed roughly, wondering what he had planned next. It was not long before Afton had her answer.

"Does it hurt here?" Lorenz inquired just prior to his tongue invading her glistening fold, already slick with her juices.

Afton screamed as his tongue penetrated. She squirmed as he continued his exploration partially embarrassed and so turned on, she never wanted him to finish what he was doing. As he flicked her nub, Afton let out another scream. She reached out for his hair, trying to pull him in closer. She wanted more, duly awarded as his tongue increased its pace.

Her orgasm hit hard an instant later. It was the first one she had without him sharing the rapture of what they produced together. Although she loved what he did to her, it felt incomplete without him sharing the experience. If he had done this before the transformation, she wondered if she would feel the same way.

He withdrew from her and brought his body to lie directly over hers. Lorenz aware of her battered body kept most of his weight on his forearms. "This time, you are on top," Lorenz said. "You know where you are injured and sore. The last thing I want is to hurt you."

She clasped her mouth to his as he gently turned them. His kiss was salve to her soul. She clasped her hand against his face as she deepened their kiss. They devoured each other, as they generated and shared energy. His engorged member rubbed against her, eager to remind Afton she was in for another ride of her life. She rained kisses over his face and neck, as she moved her body down the length of him. She licked his carotid artery as she passed the source of what had started her transformation. However, she did not want blood, she only wanted this man to make love to her.

Her hands left his face and grabbed a hold of his shoulders as she continued her journey south. She kissed and licked the muscles of his chest, enjoying the salty taste. As she worked on his chest, Lorenz's fingers dug into her hips, his urgency evident as the pressure he applied increased. He was no longer concerned about the healed blood vessels that created the bruising.

Not wanting to torture him any longer, she positioned herself over him and impaled herself on his member. They both cried out in unison. It felt so damn good, Afton could barely hold back her next orgasm. She increased the pace as she rode him, wanting him to reach the same urgency her body struggled with.

After everything they had been through today, she was amazed at the energy flowing between them. Afton had no idea of the source of the power. She knew they generated it and became stronger both physically and mentally.

As long as they had each other and the ability to have physical relations, they had an endless life-force. She continued to ride him, sweat silkening her body. Lorenz's hands glided up her slick body until he had possession of both her breasts.

She raised her hands to heaven, as if thanking a supreme being for what she had. Unable to hold back any longer, she let out one last scream. His cry joined hers as they climaxed together. A perfect moment shared as soul mates became one. Afton stayed on top of him as his hands continued to worship her body. His touch was magic, both internally and externally. He was still inside her, hard and ready for more of the enchantment they had together.

Although she had felt and enjoyed what his hands had done to her through their lovemaking, she had not looked at them. Her eyes now focused on her body and the mess that had been on his hand, which was now all over her body.

"What is that?" Afton asked.

⌒◯

Lorenz was dazed. Their love-making just got more intense every time they were together. Afton had asked him a question, but for the life of him, he had been too out of it to comprehend what she was asking.

"What was on your hands?" she asked again. "You managed to get it all over me?"

Lorenz looked at her lovely skin and saw remnants of her dried blood clinging to it. He had done such a thorough job loving her, her body was covered with the dark brown red flecks. How was he going to explain this without panicking her?

"After you fell in battle, I held you in my arms. My hands became saturated with your blood. I swore I would not wash you from my skin until you were totally recovered. Although it was clear you had recovered fully, I was too busy to clean up."

Afton looked at him, her expression blank. Tears started to roll down her cheeks, shining like little diamonds as they made their way down her face. He took one of his hands and captured a tear. He rubbed his fingers together, soaking in Afton's essence.

"I love you," she said as she lowered her torso and brought her lips once again to his.

It was the first time she had uttered those precious words. Too moved for words, he merely deepened the kiss. Once again, he was lost in her aura, too caught up with her to respond to what she said, other than with his body. He had wanted to tell her how he felt, but he did not want to repeat her sentiments immediately after she said them.

Although she had not overreacted to having her dried blood on her body, he wanted to remove it. Show her how much he felt for her by caring for her body. He gathered her in his arms, rose from their bed, and carried her to the washroom. Somehow he had managed all of that without breaking the kiss.

He reached into the shower and turned on the water. It always took forever to get the hot water flowing, the last thing he wanted was to have her body assault by cold, frigid water. When it was just right, he stepped into the invigorating jets. Afton let out a little cry when the pressure hit her legs.

"*A little warmer,*" she instructed telepathically, not wanting to release his lips. Obviously her transformation had not given her the ability to regulate her body's temperature.

After adjusting the knob, Lorenz placed her on her feet and started to wash her lovely shoulders. The dried blood came off easily, as he made his way down her body. There had been just enough blood on her skin to make the water have a light pink hue as it swirled down the drain at their feet.

It was not long before she was glistening clean. His body hungered with need for her again, now that he had cared for her. There seemed to be no saturation point when it came to his craving his soul mate.

He was leaning down to take one of her breasts into his mouth when she clasped her hands around his head and stopped his forward progress. "I have another lesson with Frazour," Afton informed him.

"You just had one," he growled, not believing his ears. He could not bear to have her body bruised again. He knew Frazour was properly preparing her, not holding back, but he did not like the side-effects on the body he worshipped.

"The risk is great and I have so much to learn, it's not even funny. Frazour just gave me enough time to have my bruises heal. Originally he was not even going to give me that. There are no breaks in war!" She said that last sentence in a failed attempt to sound like his blood brother.

"Sadly," Lorenz confessed, "the bastard is correct. Wylaine can attack at any time and I just wasted valuable time in preparing you for the attack."

Afton placed her arms around his waist and brought her breasts against his chest. "I wouldn't say what we just had together was a waste of time. It was a nice little diversion to give my mind a little rest. Besides, our time energized me. I can keep banging that tambourine a little longer."

Lorenz had no idea what she was talking about. One thing was clear, they needed to get dressed and back to preparing for his brother's attack. He did not want to be put in the position again where he was holding her bleeding body.

"I should check with Drake and see if he has heard anything from his spies." He could have done it telepathically, but Lorenz knew if he did not get away from Afton's naked body, neither of them were going anywhere for quite a while. "Take your time dressing, I will let Frazour know you will be with him shortly."

He left his soul mate wrapped in a towel, trying to comb out her tangled hair and mumbling to herself. The idea that he found her adorable still continued to surprise him. How he ended up getting such a gift was beyond him. The only thing left to do was kill the vampire who had once been his brother.

Chapter 24

~

Afton decided to heed Lorenz's advice and took her sweet time dressing. There were a number of beauty products Lenore had left. Who knew vampires liked a flowery scent when they drank from their victims? You learn something every day, she figured. After picking up a number of bottles, she decided on the lavender scented body lotion. It was a treat to spread it over her body. For the first time in her life her legs and arms had muscle definition. When they had the luxury of time, she was going to have Lorenz massage the oily lotion onto her back.

Getting into the one piece fighting outfit Frazour had given her was a lot easier than it had been taking it off. She imagined after the next sparing battle with her soul mate's blood brother, she was going to be in the same lousy shape as before. She grabbed an elastic band and started to tie back her hair. It was hopeless trying to do anything with it, especially if she was going to engage in physical activity.

Afton was still tying back her hair, when she entered the bedroom and stopped cold. There, standing next to her bed was Malice with a nefarious grin on his face. Her first reaction was to run out of the room, screaming for Lorenz at the top of her lungs. She needed to stop thinking like a human and leverage the powers she now possessed.

"Malice is in our chambers," Afton calmly informed her soul mate. *"I am not sure what he did with my guards, but I imagine it's not good. Whatever you do, don't come running down here without thinking of how you are going to deal with the traps he has laid out for you."*

"Stall him as long as you can," Lorenz responded back. *"Do not indicate in any way we have a telepathic channel between us. There is a way to link me in your head so I can hear what he is saying, as well as what you are sharing verbally. Try and find the pathway, just do not be obvious about it."*

Afton slowed her rapidly beating heart and concentrated on her telepathic gift. She needed to appear as if she was still adjusting to seeing Malice in her room and not plotting her next move against him. They had been so focused on preparing her physically for their next engagement, little time had been spent on strengthening her mental powers.

"How did you get in here?" Afton addressed the vampire before her. "Should I bother to ask how many bodies you left behind?" She put just enough fear in her voice to sound more frightened than she truly was. Afton was not the same woman who had been held captive by the monster standing before her.

Malice had not moved an inch since she entered the room, so Afton stayed perfectly still. The longer they talked, the more time, Lorenz and the others had to come up with a rescue plan. They needed to devise something that would not get them all killed. Her job was to buy them time to plan and execute Afton's rescue and Malice's capture.

"Preparation, my dear," Malice answered. "I do not take action unless I have studied the surroundings and have come up with numerous contingency plans. That is how I managed to be in your father's hive when you arrived. It had been my plan to bring down Yorik and take over his army. When you walked through that portal, all my plans changed."

"The train attack was your doing, not your minion's?"

"Do you not love that word? Yes, I have many minions, but they execute my orders. They barely have a brain between them all. Although I do not have The Creator's blood like my brother, I am the most powerful creature I have ever encountered."

Afton let out a short laugh. "Yes, you are a creature. Look at your decaying body; it's disgusting." She had not meant to say those words out loud. The last thing she wanted to do was anger him.

"Yes, I am a beast, and look at you." He did not seem emotionally impacted by her words. Emotions were traits of humanity, something Malice had little traces of. "It was a smart move to let you escape and have Lorenz finish the transformation. You are certainly something to behold. The metamorphosis was certainly beyond my expectations. What a prize I will have at my side going forward."

"The bastard has the hallway leading to our quarters totally inaccessible," Lorenz provided her an update. *"I do not know how he managed to secure it so quickly, I had just walked through the passageway not more than ten minutes prior. Are you all right?"*

"Your brother is boasting. I will keep him talking for as long as I can. Just hurry!"

She must not have properly reacted to Malice's words while she was conversing with Lorenz. He got up slowly from the bed and walked toward her. It took all her willpower to stand her ground.

"So, you have gained the gift of telepathy, how interesting," Malice observed. He looked at her as her father had earlier, trying to ascertain what other gifts she had gained. "What else can you do?"

"Guess," Afton responded. The conversation was working as a great new strategy to buy Lorenz and the others more time. Hopefully, he had a checklist like her father that Malice would slowly go through.

Malice pulled out a knife and then reached for her arm. She held her breath as Malice slashed her wrist. Afton muffled the cry of pain resulting from his attack. There was no way she was going to give him the satisfaction of letting him see he had hurt her. Her body healed the cut faster than any injury she had sustained previously. She was still growing in power, which was evident.

"Excellent," Malice said, addressing his comment more to himself than to Afton. "When we are together again, I do not have to be gentle any longer. We will see how much your body can withstand." A shiver ran down Afton's spine. He had such joy in his voice, there was not a doubt in her mind he would enjoy hurting her again and again.

She had promised herself she was not going to fall prey to this sadistic bastard again. Earlier, she had reminded herself she was not the same girl she was when he first had control of her. However, she had not tried to leverage her new gifts as a tool. It was about time she did.

In all likelihood, Afton was not going to overpower Malice with strength. The monstrosity before her had been honing his powers for eons. Afton had managed to compel Drake with little effort, perhaps Malice had used his powers more for physical strength than manipulation of the mind. There was only one way to find out. It was unlikely Lorenz and the others were going to get to her in time before Malice executed, whatever escape plan he had drawn up.

Afton took the hand he had cut and gently grabbed his chin. It took all her self-control to hide the revulsion she felt touching him. She looked him in the eyes, captivating him with her glance.

"Wouldn't it be nicer to kiss and hold each other, rather than whatever sick games you are concocting in that brain of yours?" Afton was amazed at how enticing her voice sounded.

She watched with amazement as he brought his lips forward and planted them on her own. For her charade to work, she needed to display she was not repulsed by his kiss or his touch. If her plan was to be successful, she needed to compel him into something he would never do.

As soon as he released his lips, she brought her tongue forward and licked the saliva he had left behind. Her performance was worthy of an Academy Award, as far as she was concerned. She quickly plastered a smile on her face, rather than vomiting on the floor.

"Wasn't that nicer than hurting me? We both can find pleasure in each other. I can take you to places you have never been before with another woman. After all, I am like no other girl you have ever been with or will be with again."

Afton could tell he was overwhelmed with what she was doing. The man was obsessed with her for some reason and was reacting to her without her using compulsion. So far, so good, now she just needed to continue down the road she was navigating very carefully.

It was time to blow his mind. She pulled back the cat suit from her shoulders and wiggled out of the tight material. Afton stood nude before the most dangerous being she had ever encountered. She only prayed her strategy was going to pay dividends in the end.

The weapon she used now was the most powerful she possessed, her body. She stood there proud, not embarrassed or concerned about what he would do to her. Control belonged to Afton and she was going to leverage it to destroy Malice.

"Look at how I have changed, Malice," she said as she slowly turned around. "Lorenz made this possible, but it is your touch I miss. You worshiped my body like no one had ever before. I long for your fingers to once again bring me to life." She was probably pouring it on too thick, but he seemed to like that.

She came forward and brought one of his hands to her breast. When he started to squeeze on it, she let out moans of encouragement. He shifted their positions and led her back toward the bed.

"No," she said, once again making eye contact with Malice. "I share this bed with your brother. The sheets are soiled with his scent. There is a place I want to take you even Lorenz does not have the strength to go. Let's make love for the first time in my very special spot. You want that, don't you?"

"Yes," Malice answered. "You will allow me to make love to you?"

"I am counting on it," Afton answered. She needed to continue to reinforce the compulsion as they moved closer to where she would finally put an end to this monster. "You want to make love to me where Lorenz has not touched me. It can become our special place."

Afton took his hand and walked toward the secret entrance to the courtyard. She figured halfway to their destination Malice would weaken and perhaps would be easier to manipulate. There was also the possibility he would realize what she had planned and kill her with his bare hands.

They reached the secret entrance and Afton lit a set of candles before they entered. Her hand had quaked a bit as she lit the match, she hoped Malice had not noticed the tremor. She turned to smile at him, once again captivating his attention.

"Let's walk side by side, so we can gaze into each other's eyes. The passage is narrow, but we can snuggle as we walk."

Together they entered, Afton holding the candles and Malice's hand clasped to her hip. She did not close the entryway, incase Lorenz finally broke through the traps Malice had set for him. In all likelihood, she would continue to be on her own.

"You want to love me where I can lie on soft, beautiful grass." Afton maintained eye contact with Malice.

"Actually," Malice sneered, "right here would be a perfect place to continue our sessions until the sun sets and we will escape through the courtyard you were so anxious to get me to." He shoved her and came down hard on top of her. "Did you really think you could compel me into the sun?"

Malice grabbed the candlesticks that had fallen after he had attacked, throwing them out of her reach. She was weaponless against a vampire more powerful than Drake, Lorenz, and possibly her father. Afton was not going to give him the satisfaction of falling apart and giving him an easy victory.

"What do you hope to gain from possessing me?" Afton spit out at him. "Did you get one ounce of power when you kissed me? Only my soul mate can feed power from me and you are not my soul mate. I am just another reminder that your brother once again got the better deal. Lorenz received immortality from The Creator and a soul mate. What have you got?"

"Shut up," Malice screamed at her.

"Wylaine, you are never going to outdo your brother. You are pathetic, while he is beautiful."

"My name is Malice, call me by the proper name."

"No, your name is Wylaine. You are alone, while I belong to your brother. He has four blood brothers who are loyal to him. Who do you have?"

"I have heard enough, you will shut that mouth of yours."

"Make me, you bastard."

Wylaine brought his hand around her throat, choking her so she could no longer goad him with the truth. She should not have taunted him as she had done. He was too strong for her to physically stand a chance against him.

They were at the spot where Lorenz had told her he used to start feeling fatigue from the sun. Frazour had told her The Creator could manipulate the elements and perhaps one day she would as well. Now was as good as any to see what she was capable of doing.

Afton concentrated on the warmth of the sun and how she loved how it caused snow to sparkle. She could feel it beating down on her back during the summer, on the rare occasions she wore a halter top. She concentrated on the sun, as Wylaine strangled her. Well, if she died, she would have her final vision be the sun. How she wished she had made love to Lorenz under the golden orb.

Energy started to course through her at the thought of her soul mate and the sun. She was a conduit of the element and could soak in its energy. Heat started to spread through her body.

"What are you doing?" Wylaine screamed. "Stop it!"

Afton continued to think of her soul mate and the beating heat of the sun. She could feel the choke hold Wylaine had against her throat weaken. There was still capacity within her to take in more of the power of the one thing that weakened vampires.

Her body was throbbing with solar energy. Wylaine screamed as he lifted himself off her and started to crawl away. It had been a stroke of genius when she had stripped off her clothing. There was no material to absorb the power she emitted. She launched herself on the back of Lorenz's brother and used her strength not to fight him, but to bare him to her power.

"Where are you, Afton?" Lorenz frantically asked through their channel. *"We finally made it through to our chamber and you are nowhere in sight."*

"I have everything under control," she answered. *"We are in the passageway to the courtyard. You can join me, but warn the others to stay in our chamber. I have found a new power, the energy of the sun."*

Depleted of most of his power, Wylaine barely moved below her. Not wanting to take any chances, Afton still harnessed more energy and brought it down onto her victim. Now was not the time to back off and show mercy.

Lorenz made the short distance to where she lay in record time. "What do you need me to do?"

"Let me turn over with Wylaine, then pick us up, sandwiching your brother between the two of us. I will keep him weak with the power of the sun until we can get him outside and have it finish him off. You can say goodbye to your brother as he becomes a pile of ash."

No words greeted her plan, just action. Her soul mate lifted them both after she rolled onto her back. Lorenz carried them the rest of the way to the courtyard and then hesitated when they reached the door to the unprotected area outside.

"Wylaine?" Lorenz asked. There was anguish in his voice. After all the years that had passed, it was clear to Afton that her soul mate still loved his brother.

"She is right," Wylaine replied weakly, "you win, brother of mine. You were a better man, a better vampire, and now it appears her soul mate. Finish what you should have done a long time ago. Do one last show of brotherly love; end my miserable existence."

Afton could see acceptance in Lorenz's eyes. He would do what The Creator had always known he would do, end the life of the creature who had once been his brother.

Whatever Wylaine had once felt for his brother, he dug deep and gave him one last gift. Lorenz would not carry the guilt of killing the boy he once played with as a child. She tightened her grip on her soul mate as he carried the three of them into the light of day.

Chapter 25

～

They showered separately, washing off the dust that had once been Lorenz's brother. Wylaine was now out of their lives. She could finally call him by his given name as she had toward the end of his life. He no longer held any power over her.

Lorenz had left their chamber as soon as he had dressed. She knew he did not carry the guilt associated with his brother's death; however, he had mourned the boy he had grown up with. Whatever space he needed, she would give it to him, including the closeness soul mates could provide during the healing process if he desired it. She would not push herself on him, but provide the companionship he would possibly crave.

A party from the Troyk universe would be arriving soon, she needed to get her act together and finish dressing. Afton did not want to miss an opportunity to spend time with Shirl. She never had any close friends growing up on Earth, maybe she could develop one with the crystal telepath who could travel between worlds.

When she finally made it to the center hall, she discovered the Troyk visitors had already arrived. Shirl and Alex came forward to greet her. To Afton's surprise, both women embraced her. It was a wonderful feeling to know someone other than Lorenz cared for her.

"Wow! Look at you." Shirl's eyes were large with surprise. "Your father said you would go through some kind of transformation to save your life, but wow, this is more than I ever dreamed possible."

"It was all a little overwhelming at first, I have to admit. My body changed overnight, but my powers continue to develop and grow."

Shirl laughed, "We have to compare notes someday. I will tell you about mine, if you tell me about yours. Just be careful, Alex can read minds, so she'll probably know before I do."

"Alex, what are you doing here?" Afton asked. She noticed Drake was not hovering, which was a good sign, but stood with the men several yards away. "You need to stay away from Drake, for the sake of the baby."

Alex turned and looked over her shoulder. She was probably just double checking Drake's proximity to her, as well as to see where her soul mate was. "Benko Jarlyn, our future leader, has made a deal with Drake to provide him with crystals, as well as take care of a vendetta he has against your father. Turns out, I am part of the deal." Alex did not seem upset by the bargain struck with Drake. It was not too long ago Afton had to cope with agreements made relating to her own life.

Her father had headed back to his hive as soon as Wylaine had been dispatched. To her surprise, he embraced her and kissed her forehead before he left. Maybe there was still hope that one day she would have a relationship with her father. With her company present, Afton was happy Yorik had left.

"What value could crystals have that would make Benko accept such ridiculous terms?" It was beyond reasonable as far as Afton was concerned.

"We have no idea," Shirl replied. "I use them to travel between worlds and they are used to fuel our weapons, beyond that I do not have a clue. Benko wants them as badly as his father does, so there has to be more regarding the power of the stones I am not familiar with. Tarsea has given Drake approval to visit with Alex as long as he is there. There is also talk of him coming into the Troyk universe for some of the visitations."

The idea of welcoming a vampire in that world was frightening. Drake seemed trustworthy, but the Troyk people were taking a lot of risk for some rocks. She wondered if anyone beyond the small group of friends and their future leader were aware of the upcoming trips.

"I have been having terrible morning sickness," Alex confessed, "but everything seems to right itself when the baby is in proximity to Drake. We try not to think about the ramifications of all this. Seeing you has really eased my mind. Frankly, I am not sure what to think, the whole thing is freaking me out.

I have asked that you are also present when I visit with Drake, even in the Troyk universe, if that is all right."

She was overjoyed by the request. "Let me discuss it with Lorenz," Afton answered, "but I am sure he will not have an issue with it. It would be cool to visit other worlds." Afton reached out and touched Shirl's crystals. "I cannot believe you and Darden can manipulate the portals between worlds by just using crystals and your telepathic abilities."

"Speaking of other worlds," Shirl said, "is there anything we can bring you? Based on my experience, the Nightshade universe is lacking in all sorts of things."

Afton blurted out the first thing that came to her mind. "Hair detangler and conditioner would be great. Whatever Alex uses will be fine. Lorenz had put something on my hair, but it just didn't do the trick. With all the great changes to my body and abilities, I seem to keep dwelling on my poor hair."

Shirl laughed, "We are talking about hair and babies, while the men are probably talking about battle strategies. When did our lives become a cliché?"

Alex and Afton just looked at Shirl as if she was crazy. All three women had been through so much since entering the portal to another universe, although Afton's road was a lot rockier. It only reinforced she wanted to stay in contact with these women. With The League still a threat, it was also an advantage to have off-world allies.

When Afton thought about The League, Emma came to mind. She had promised the girl a visiting crystal telepath would return her to Earth. No time like the present to make it a reality.

"There is a woman here from San Diego who fell into the Nightshade universe I would like returned to Earth. Can you manage it before you head home?"

Shirl was quick to answer. "Of course, I cannot think of anything I would rather do than liberate someone from this terrible world. You have an open invitation whenever you have had enough of this bleak place."

Afton motioned for a servant to come over and she requested Emma be brought to the great hall. Lenore had been watching over Emma like a mother hen. Afton figured her friend would miss the girl after she left. There were probably countless women in this world who needed their help. With her new powers continuing to evolve, Afton could not imagine a better way to use them than to rescue abused women from vampires.

"We have to go," Starc came over to inform Shirl.

"Not just yet," Shirl replied. "We are waiting for someone we are going to take to Ginkgo Terra before we return home." Starc raised an eyebrow, but did not cross-examine his soul mate.

Emma entered the room and was brought directly to Afton. She hugged the girl. "Time to go home. This is the woman I told you about who can navigate the portal back to Earth." For the first time since she had known Emma, the girl smiled. It was the type of smile that lit up the room.

Lorenz came up from behind and whispered in her ear, "We have to talk."

Afton wanted Emma safely on her way before anything happened. "Can we discuss this later? I want to wish the Troyk people and Emma a safe journey."

"Unfortunately not," Lorenz answered. "Emma is not going anywhere." She grabbed his sleeve and the two of them walked away from the small group of people gathered in front of the area where Shirl would soon open a portal.

"What are you talking about?" Afton blurted out as soon as they had a little privacy.

"Emma cannot leave the Nightshade universe. A deal was struck involving her."

"What is it between you men and deals? Don't you realize you are impacting lives you have no business imposing upon? Who did you make the deal with and for what?" Afton was close to losing her patience. With her heightened powers, she wondered how they would react to anger. "Let me guess, this has something to do with Frazour."

"As soon as Frazour saw Emma, he knew she was his other half," Lorenz informed her. Afton looked between the small, timid girl and the brute of a vampire. Those two certainly did not belong together, he could easily crush her between his mammoth hands. "His price to aid us was Emma. The agreement was sealed in blood, I cannot go back on the promise I made."

How was she going to break through to him? "You just can't give a person over to another as if they were property! Besides, I did not make any such promise, other than to Emma to get her out of this world."

"Anyone in this settlement indirectly belongs to me," Lorenz was losing his patience now it seemed. "Your father gave you to me. Same thing applies here."

Afton stood there mute, not knowing how to reply to him. Everything he said was true, she had no power over her life in this world and it appeared the same was true related to Emma. She struggled with what she was going to have to tell the poor woman.

"You will make a liar out of me," she whispered, not really caring if he heard her or not. She knew she had lost this battle before the first shot was fired.

"Better a liar, then dead," Lorenz growled. "I would have done anything I could to keep you alive. Unfortunately for Emma, she was one of the prices it took this time around."

Lorenz rejoined the group. Afton could not hear what was being said, but she knew her soul mate was explaining the fate the Nightshade universe had in store for Emma. Shirl looked in her direction and Afton could only nod her acceptance. Emma ran out of the room in tears. She wished she could follow the girl and comfort her, but she did not have the words, not that they would be believed, after her first promise had been broken.

She watched as the Troyk citizens left through the portal, free of the human politics, she was now neck deep in. Afton felt helpless and worn down. It seemed with every step forward she made, she ended up taking two steps backwards. One day, when her powers had matured, she would right the wrongs done today. Right now, she was helpless to do anything other than acquiesce.

Chapter 26

Afton took another sip of her wine, letting the liquid seep down her throat. Her nose burned with the aftertaste of the beverage. She leaned her head back, letting the warmth gradually work its way through her body. Lorenz grabbed her hand and an altogether different heat brewed from within. She sensed her soul mate wanted to head to bed, but Afton wanted to languish here a little longer. Just a couple more minutes of peace before Lorenz reawakened her body's urges.

They had sex after Shirl and her friends left. Both were angry and depleted, in need of restoring their energy. It was the first time they came together for just the purpose of feeding, neither of them saying a word. She knew they would work past this particular issue, they loved each other too much to stay mad too long. Afton knew she was going to have to relent on this problem. She was not going to change the customs of the Nightshade universe overnight.

A loud crackling sound vibrated through the room, causing Afton to sit straight up. The air snapped with static. What in the world was going on? Afton had seen portals open and they did not generate this much natural disruption. For a moment she feared some kind of weapon was going to explode.

Just prior to ducking underneath the table, Afton saw a gateway of spiraling air open. An impressive man and woman exited the portal. She was taken aback by the power both of them generated. Their energy sucked up the electricity she had noted in the air earlier.

Lorenz, Drake, and Frazour rose from their chairs to greet their visitors. Before he left her side Lorenz placed his hand on her shoulder, communicating she should stay seated. To her surprise, all three men fell to their knees before the man.

"My sons," the man said. This could not possibly be who she thought he was. The Creator had disappeared thousands of years ago. Her eyes shifted to the beautiful woman next to him. She was like Afton, a soul mate who transformed into another being. The tall blonde was elegant, dressed in a long flowing white gown.

Her soul mate was the first to find his voice. "Master, it is an honor to welcome you and your mate. May I introduce you to my soul mate, Afton?" Lorenz acted like they had only been separated for a couple of years, rather than thousands. Obviously, she was not handling it quite the same way, she was still stunned.

"That is why we have momentarily returned," the female responded. "The first of our children has found his mate. We have come to rescue you both from this world."

"What?" Afton said as she sprung up from the table and ran to Lorenz's side.

"Neither of you belong here any longer," she addressed Afton. Her power was overwhelming, Afton felt herself weaken as the woman absorbed her power.

"Our apologies," The Creator said, "in our world the elements are neutralized, preventing us from pulling power seeping from others. There are beings there like ourselves, living among the people who originally settled there."

It sounded like Shangri-La, straight out of James Hilton's novel. How she would have loved to go to a mystical, harmonious world, but she had unfinished work here. Afton could not help but see the look on Lorenz's face as he glanced between his two blood brothers.

"Creator," Afton started, she was not sure what to call him. "You bestow upon us a great honor. Nothing would please me more than to join you one day. But I have dedicated myself for the time being to help people from other worlds who find themselves enslaved here.

"The powers bestowed on me and my soul mate must have been gifted upon us to do more than lie in a beautiful world in lounges, eating grapes. Besides, it will not be the right time until all of your children have transcended. When all of Lorenz's blood brothers have found their soul mates, then we will join you. In the meantime, they need us, as does the Nightshade universe. This world needs to change and we have the power to make it happen."

The Creator came forward and took Afton's face in his hands and kissed her lips gently. The power he transferred was nothing like what moved between her and Lorenz. It was pure energy at its roughest state. She stumbled backwards as soon as The Creator released her, only to be captured in her soul mate's arms.

"A woman worthy of one of my sons," The Creator finally said after Afton righted herself.

The Creator's soul mate took a step forward and took both Afton's and Lorenz's hands. "With the transformation, you have the ability to control the elements of your world. Through your manipulation of air, earth, water, and fire you both have the ability to travel between worlds together. Learn this power and come to us as a united party when you have all entered the next stage of existence."

"Until that time, my children…" The Creator said before the elemental gateway opened again and both of them stepped through it.

The room was quiet as the last sputter of energy waned.

Afton collapsed on to her soul mate's chest. The energy The Creator had shared with her had been so overpowering, she had to share it with Lorenz. They had spent the last six hours exchanging energy back and forth, nearly killing themselves in the process.

"I wonder what their world is like," Afton finally had the ability to speak.

"A gluttonous world from what I can tell," Lorenz said as he turned on his side, bringing her with him. "If sex and feeding is anything like what we just experienced, no one would ever leave their homes. Not that I am complaining, but the loss of control was a bit scary. There were times I was afraid I was going to hurt you." He gently brushed her curly hair out of her face.

"You would never hurt me," Afton shared with him. "There was a time I was so weak I could barely stand, but you never attempted to overpower me. Now, I think I can hold my own against you."

"Never against me, love," Lorenz muttered as he kissed her. "I was struck by you the minute I saw you. Both physically by what I imagined you would become and the strength of spirit you showed, as your father tried to get you to cower. Even before I realized we were soul mates, I wanted you like nothing I had ever wanted during my entire existence. I finally have found love and I am totally overwhelmed by you."

Afton smiled, she could not help it. This man might own her because of the contract he entered with her father, but she gave him her heart willingly. When she had been given the opportunity to escape this world, she realized she could not leave him. He had become her world, regardless of what physical plane they resided in.

"Do you think Emma is Frazour's soul mate? They look so wrong together," Afton admitted.

"I suppose the same could be said for what we looked like side by side originally. I wanted to throttle Drake when he started to flirt with you."

"Drake, now there is a piece of work. That baby is not even born yet, how can he possibly know she is his soul mate? Did you know I was yours when my mother was pregnant with me?"

"Alex and the baby are telepathic, you were not until the transformation," Lorenz explained. "I imagine had you been, you would have communicated with me, as the baby has to Drake. Instead, you slipped past my fingers into a world I could not enter without assistance. Had your father not been ruthless in his quest to have you returned, I shudder to think what would have happened."

"What are the odds the soul mates for your remaining brothers are nearby? I spent most of my life on Earth and had Alex not come to Nightshade, her baby would have been born in the Troyk universe, none the wiser. The whole thing is mind blowing."

"In the meantime, I have called my other two blood brothers to join us. The five of us have not been together for thousands of years. What information we have to share, after all this time, I cannot imagine."

"Just promise me you will safeguard their soul mates from your brothers. There is to be no strong arming or intimidating these women, especially Emma."

"That will be my second priority."

"Lorenz, what is your first?"

"You, silly girl. You are the love of my immortal life and I have spent all of it so far without you. I have a lot of time to make up for."

Afton once again lost herself in his kiss. How could such a terrible beginning, end so happily? She wrapped her arms around her soul mate. Energy sparked between them. They had all the time in the world and she knew how she wanted to spend the next several millennia.

The End

Enjoy the 1st Chapter of 'The Chameleon Soul Mate'
Worlds Apart Series: Book One

Chapter 1

~

Arizona

Alexandra Mann, 'Alex' to friends and foes, disconnected from the call center system and let out a long, painful sigh. People never called to comment on how great things were, just to complain.

But she had the ability to stay calm under pressure and deal with any situation. Didn't matter if it was a customer yelling or her two best friends coming to her with their latest crisis. Alex took whatever life threw at her and made lemon drop cocktails.

Finally Friday was here and Alex was going up to Sedona with three friends. They had been planning this trip for five months, and the countdown was finally over. This weekend was a double celebration: her twenty-first birthday and her best friend Shirl's twenty-third.

She had actually taken a half day of vacation so she and Shirl could get a jump on the traffic that headed north every Friday afternoon. Two of her co-workers were joining them, but had to work all day and would drive up later.

She grabbed her purse and pulled out her phone. The display showed that Shirley Tomlinson called. Shirl, as she liked to be called, had grown up with Alex at a local Phoenix orphanage. Although Alex was younger than Shirl, they were best friends and as close as sisters. Shirl and Candy, who also grew up with them at the orphanage, were Alex's only family. The three were connected, at times it felt like they could read each other's minds.

Alex had given up on the dream of a real family long before the orphanage stopped parading her in front of perspective parents. Years of couples talking and playing with her, only to have them walk away, had taken their toll. The disappointment she felt at the continual rejection caused her to cry herself to sleep on many occasions. She would find herself blending into the shadows, in order not to be passed over again.

To this day, she had a tendency to blend into the background. Her best friends were always in the spotlight, where Alex tended to be invisible in their presence. Shirl was tall, blond, and stop traffic gorgeous. Candy, on the other hand, had a self-confidence that made her radiant. When they were together, both men and women would flock to Candy.

Having left her cubical, Alex took the opportunity to listen to Shirl's voice mail message. "Alex, it's Shirl. I've got a killer migraine and I can't make it to Sedona this weekend."

If anyone else had canceled on her, she would have been angry. However, she knew Shirl got terrible migraines that would down a small elephant. It seemed as though the headaches were growing in frequency and she was concerned about her friend. Alex recently started having migraines herself. She and Shirl were so close, she felt they were probably sympathy headaches.

When Alex reached the call center's lobby, she called Shirl before she walked out into the Arizona heat.

"What?" Shirl growled as the call connected.

"How are you feeling? Do you need anything?" Alex asked.

"Can you get me a new brain?"

"Doubtful, but I'll look into it. I am so sorry you won't make it to Sedona with us."

"I know, Alex," Shirl's voice began to fade. "Candy will stop by before she takes her class on this weekend's field trip. Don't worry, I will be fine."

Shirl hung up before Alex could say anything more. Alex placed her phone in her purse and walked toward her car in the stifling Arizona heat. The car was all packed and ready to go for the trip up to Sedona. Since she was not picking up Shirl, she immediately got on I-17 and headed north.

Alex loved Sedona and started thinking about what types of adventures she'd have this weekend. Something unusual always happened when she was there. It was odd, she was never able to put into words what she experienced. Some invisible force always seemed to draw her.

⌒੭

Alex made good time. Leaving Phoenix early afternoon was the trick, beating the hordes of commuters heading home after work. She headed straight to her hotel.

It would be some time before her call center friends would join her. In the meantime, Alex had time to hike in Boynton Canyon. She opened her suitcase, pulled out a T-shirt and shorts.

The Boynton Canyon Vortex was one of the four vortexes that contributed to the energy felt throughout Sedona. Alex generally hike Boynton Canyon because she felt the best energy there and enjoyed the trails. A lot was written about Sedona's vortexes, including the belief the energy was the result of inter dimensional gateways. She did not believe all that nonsense, but her friend Shirl certainly did. With that thought, Alex felt the loss of Shirl not being there. She could almost visualize her friend standing next to her, clutching her crystal necklaces.

She walked to her car and made the short trip between the hotel and Boynton Canyon. The parking lot closest to the trail was packed. Fortunately, she had the world's smallest car and found a spot where someone had parked badly, leaving only three quarters of a space. She easily fit into the spot and patted the dashboard of her beloved car. It was fire engine red, with a white racing stripe down the side. She loved zipping around town.

Alex changed from her sneakers into her hiking boots, locked the car and made her way to the trail head. She loved the sound her boots made against the gravel trail. Alex had just purchased a new pair of hiking boots as a birthday present to herself. The boots almost came up a quarter of her leg and were kind of clunky. She was not going to take any chances if she came across a snake along the trail.

Although the lot had been full, she didn't see anyone on the trail. A flash of light caught her eye. It was the reflection coming off a bracelet worn by someone suddenly ahead of her. Her eyes left the cuff bracelet to the man who wore it. He was tall with blond hair, and she couldn't help but admire his body. The man was oddly dressed for hiking. It appeared he was wearing a tunic and leggings. He had broad shoulders underneath the blue tunic and the leggings were molded to his powerful legs. She could see the muscle definition of his legs even from this distance. He must have decided to take a little hike before performing in a Shakespearean play. Sedona was known for supporting all art forms.

Alex admired his body, but unfortunately her body was not reacting to his. It never did, regardless how attractive she found the man. Oddly, Shirl and Candy had the same problem. She dated, because girls her age dated. She had not been with a man in over six months. Every relationship was disappointing when it became physical. The guys she dated didn't want to sustain a relationship if they had to deal with an ice queen in bed.

As she continued on the path, she kept an eye on the man, closing the gap between them. He was carrying a number of sacks that seemed to slow him down. Another oddity about the man. Who carried sacks on a day hike, rather than a backpack?

He was in her sight one minute and the next he vanished. Where did he go? Alex ran forward, thinking the man had fallen and needed help. She arrived at the spot where she had last seen him and there was no sign of him.

An invisible force pulled her forward, off her feet. She screamed as the motion continued and her vision went black. Her lungs seized and she fell into what she could only think was an endless void.

Savior the 1ˢᵗ Chapter of 'The Crystal Telepath'
Worlds Apart Series: Book One

Chapter 1

⁓

Sedona, Arizona

She exited the car, so weak she could barely close the door. The remnants of the second migraine this week had left her feeling lethargic. Shirl Tomlinson knew she had to power through, regardless of how dreadful she was feeling. Her best friend, Alexandra Mann, had been missing for almost a week. As she walked to the front of the Sedona Police Department headquarters, she was oblivious to the beauty of the surrounding area. Several people exiting the building made way for Shirl as she entered. She barely noticed their presence or the way the men perused her body. She was too sick to care.

For a relatively small town, the place was extremely busy. Barely able to stand, she staggered toward the front desk. She had to dodge a number of officers; otherwise, she would have ended up flat on her face on the marble floor. The man who stood behind the counter saw her distress and made his way around the restricted area to aid her. The artificial light was so bright, she had to squint her eyes as she watched him approach.

"Miss Tomlinson, are you all right?" the concerned officer asked. Shirl wished she could remember the young officer's name. He was wearing a name badge, but her vision was blurry and she could not make out the letters. She just wanted to crawl into the corner and fall into a deep, painless sleep.

"I am recovering from a migraine and am not feeling quite right," she said. One severe headache after another had tapped her strength. She did not know how much more she was going to be able to take. Having only minimal health insurance coverage, her options were limited in her quest to find what was wrong with her. Every doctor she saw scratched their heads, baffled by the escalation in the severity and frequency of the headaches she had been suffering the past two years.

"I'll get Commander Lewis. He will give you an update on our efforts to find your friend." The officer took a couple of steps and then asked over his shoulder, "Can I get you any water?"

Shirl shook her head. She had taken medication before she left the hotel room. Everyone in the Sedona Police Department knew her by now. She arrived on Monday, as soon as she was able to drive. Alex had been missing since last Friday. For three full days, the police station had been her home away from home.

She sat on the bench, clasping the crystals that hung around her neck. As each day ended with no sign of Alex, Shirl got more frantic, fearing she would never see her friend again. What would she do without Alex in her life? They had grown up together in a Phoenix orphanage. Whenever anything went wrong, she always ran to Alex for help. Although Alex was two years younger, Alex was always the responsible one.

Commander Lewis appeared and sat next to Shirl. He was a good looking man, probably in his late thirties. The man was also tall. Generally she had to look up at him when they talked, she liked that. For some odd reason, she did not trust men she had to look down upon. She knew that was stupid, but that was how she felt.

Lewis was the second highest ranking police officer in the department, under the chief of police. Shirl could see from the expression on his face, he did not have good news to share. At least they hadn't found a body. The last two nights Shirl had woken in a cold sweat, dreaming she'd been taken to the morgue to identify Alex's corpse.

"I don't know what to tell you, Miss Tomlinson. There have been no sightings of your friend. We know she checked into her hotel Friday afternoon and was not seen again. Her car was found in a parking lot near Boynton Canyon. We believe she went hiking, but there are no signs of foul play. We have had men up and down that canyon looking for Alexandra. There was a part of the trail that looked like someone was dragged for ten feet or so, but there is no evidence she fell. Why don't you head home? I'll call you if we discover anything."

Shirl felt tears falling down her cheeks and reached into her purse for a tissue. "I can't leave here without Alex or knowing what happened to her." People did not just disappear off the face of the Earth. Sedona seemed an unlikely place for human trafficking. A new age cult perhaps, but Alex wasn't the type.

"Can I at least take you to dinner? You look terrible." Shirl had to smile at Commander Lewis's comment. Men usually fawned over her. It was nice to have a man be honest with her about her appearance. He was a no nonsense guy, saying what was on his mind.

She didn't feel threatened by him. Commander Lewis was the type of man to drag his wife along, eliminating any type of impropriety. It would be nice to get her mind off Alex, even for one meal. "That would be nice. I can't remember the last time I ate." She had a couple of power bars in her car, but hadn't been able to stomach the idea of eating them.

"Why don't I pick you up tonight in your hotel lobby after I get off, around seven." The seasoned police officer knew this meet-up location would be non-threatening compared to meeting her at her hotel room. "My wife Carol will meet us at the restaurant." Yup, she called that one right!

"I guess at this point, I should at least ask your first name," Shirl said. "It would be weird calling your wife Carol while calling you Commander Lewis."

"Frank, my first name is Frank."

Commander Lewis patted her hand and returned to work. She watched as he crossed into the restricted area behind the front desk. A large clock displayed three o'clock. She had four hours to kill before he would pick her up. There was no sense staying on the hard bench. She could get an update at dinner tonight. Besides, they had her cell phone number if they found Alex in the meantime.

Shirl walked to her car and sat behind the wheel for a while, not sure where she wanted to go. The medication had kicked in and she felt a little better.

She started toward Boynton Canyon. Shirl rarely went hiking with Alex. She didn't like the dust that covered her on the few occasions she went. Alex didn't make a big deal out of having to go alone.

Generally their friend Candy was along and she would hike with Alex. Candy had grown up in the orphanage with them. It was hard not calling her to join Shirl in Sedona while she waited for news of Alex. Candy was a high school coach and her team had just returned from a tournament. She hadn't even told Candy that Alex was missing. Shirl didn't want to worry her friend in case Alex reappeared. That possibility continued to slip away.

When she arrived, the parking lot was relatively empty. Alex's disappearance had been all over the local newspapers. People were shying away from this particular trail, afraid a wild animal had attacked her friend. There was no evidence to support the claim, but that did not stop the rumor mill from spreading that story.

Boynton Canyon was beautiful with its deep red rocks. Shirl had always been fascinated by this place. It was one of the four vortexes Sedona was famous for. The energy emitted by the vortexes always renewed her.

These sites were believed to be multiple dimensional pathways emitting spiraling spiritual energy. Shirl soaked up any article on the subject as well as anything dealing with mystical powers.

One of the few items she had from her birthmother was an amethyst crystal that started her fascination with crystals and healing stones. She wore four to five crystals a day, depending on her mood. Her mother's amethyst was the only crystal she wore constantly. It seemed to balance her in some odd way. Shirl felt less alone, like having family close by. She knew it was stupid, but maybe one day it would lead her to some discovery of who she was meant to be.

Curiosity about the section of the trail with the drag mark Commander Lewis mentioned got the better of Shirl. Grabbing a power bar, she started toward the trailhead. She'd walk the path Alex had taken when she disappeared. If she got too dusty, she'd take a shower before Frank picked her up for dinner.

She walked slowly, conserving what strength she had. Between nibbling on the nutrition bar, the medication, and the vortex's energy, she felt vitality coursing through her body. As she walked the trail, she held onto her crystals, trying to channel Alex. She was not expecting anything to happen, then her mother's amethyst started to glow.

Shirl held the crystal in front of her and stared at it in wonder. As much as she knew about crystals, she had never read anything about them glowing. She felt a slight pull and stopped.

The air ahead shimmered and she felt the continued emission of energy. Slowly, she approached the anomaly. She could see the trail on the other side of the air displacement.

Shirl looked down and noticed the dirt and foliage along the path looked as if something had been dragged through it. It ended right in front of what she could only think was an event horizon. Alex must have been pulled through the point of no return. The gravitational pull would have been so great, Alex would not have been able to escape from it.

Taking a deep breath, Shirl walked into the unknown.

⌒◌

Inside a black void, she felt as if falling. Twisting and turning, she had no control. Deafening, high-pitched sound pierced her ears. Her crystal glowed brighter.

Terror taking hold, she attempted to grab her crystal necklace. After her second attempt at regaining use of her flailing arms, she secured the amethyst in her hand.

Just short of all-out panic, she started to think about home. It worked for Dorothy in Oz, allowing her and Toto to return to Kansas.

She crashed against the ground, out of the portal's grasp. Shirl slowly climbed to her feet and realized she was no longer in Sedona. It must have been a portal to another dimension. That could be the only explanation why she was no longer on the trail surrounded by red rocks and dirt.

She stood on a mountain path, overlooking a city built of pale stone. The community was abloom with purple flowering trees and plants. The violet sky must be a result of the colored pollen emitted.

Shirl was surprised her mind was reacting rationally, although she was still a little dazed. Her normal reaction would have been to panic. Instead, she was taking in her surroundings and making scientific assumptions. She could not remember the last time she had thought so clearly. There was no pain or pressure impacting her brain.

Alexandra was somewhere in this city, she was certain of it. Shirl was not sure how she was going to find her or what type of people she would encounter. But she had to start looking.

She started down the mountain pass, paying close attention to her steps. The trail was steeper than the one in Boynton Canyon. Her sandals were comfortable, but not equipped to traverse the rocky path. She was also a little wobbly from the rough ride within the portal and had eaten no food to speak of for days.

Sweat trickled down her neck. She brushed at the liquid and her hand came back covered in blood. Shirl felt the same trickle on the other side of her neck. She was bleeding from both ears.

Another step. Bright red streamed from her noise. Her shirt collar was soaked with blood. A strong wave of nausea washed over her. She grabbed a tree branch along the trail.

Leaning on the tree did not abate the nausea. She fell to her knees and retched along the side of the trail. With little food and nothing to drink, it was closer to dry heaves.

Voices and footsteps were coming closer. Eyes popping open, she glanced through a red haze. Not only was she bleeding from her ears and nose, blood vessels must have broken in her eyes.

Shirl could hear the two men address her, but could not comprehend what they said. Her ears were buzzing and she could barely concentrate through the nausea that still overwhelmed her. One of the men knelt next to her as she felt herself fall into unconsciousness.

Become captivated by the 1st Chapter of 'The Warrior Woman'
Worlds Apart Series: Book Three

Chapter 1

Gingko Terra/Earth

Candy Phillips was going to kill her two best friends. She wasn't sure how, but proficient in self-defense, she could inflict serious damage to the human body. Whatever method, it was going to have to be slow and deliberate. They were going to suffer as she had suffered the last two weeks. Her friends had vanished and she had been frantic. The Sedona police department was clueless related to what had happened.

She had just purchased her third box of facial tissue since arriving in Sedona when Shirl called. Shirley Tomlinson, Shirl, disappeared while searching for their mutual friend Alexandra Mann.

All three women had grown up together in a Phoenix orphanage and were closer than most biological sisters Candy knew. It hurt that Shirl had not even informed her of Alex's disappearance. Candy had returned from taking her high school volleyball team to a tournament to find they were both missing. Candy had been crying non-stop since she arrived.

She never cried.

A feeling of abandonment she had not experienced since she was a little girl overwhelmed her. Last night she tossed and turned, unable to sleep. Her mind kept running horrible scenarios over and over again about what could have happened to her friends. Now, out of nowhere, Shirl called to request she meet her at a nearby restaurant. And that she not contact the local authorities. What kind of trouble had they gotten into?

Candy pulled into the restaurant's parking lot. At three o'clock in the afternoon, plenty of spots were open. She stopped in a space on the far side of the building. Candy needed to cool down before she saw Shirl.

Tears were once again flowing. She reached for the next box of tissues, pulled off the cardboard cover and grabbed a couple to blow her nose. She wasn't sure if she was crying because she was furious or so relieved that she could now fall apart. Either way, the fountain of tears kept flowing.

Candy had purchased a chocolate bar at the drug store as well. She tore off the wrapper and broke off a couple squares. If chocolate couldn't make her feel better, nothing would. She popped a few pieces of the creamy, dark goodness into her mouth. Leaning her head against the headrest, she closed her eyes for a moment. After collecting herself, she was ready to confront her friend.

There was not a doubt in her mind she looked a mess. Her eyes were probably swollen and her nose red from continual blowing. She needed to clean herself up before she met up with Shirl.

She pulled the elastic from what was left of her ragged ponytail. Her hair was her one vanity. With all the sports she played, it would have been so much easier if she had cut it short. Instead, she let it grow past the small of her back. Maneuvering around the steering wheel, she quickly braided it then was as ready as she ever would be to re-unite with her friend.

Slamming the car door had released some of her pent-up aggravation. It shouldn't have felt so good to abuse her poor car. As she made her way to the entrance, she took several deep, cleansing breaths. The wooden door was heavier than it looked. She put more of her weight's strength into opening it, one of the few advantages of being a big girl. The extra energy she expended further reduced her annoyance with Shirl.

As she entered, her eyes were immediately drawn to a middle-aged man. He was very attractive with his sable-colored hair and light brown eyes. The gray wisps around his temples gave him a look of sophistication. She wasn't normally attracted to older men, but this man was noteworthy.

Her eyes basked in the sight of him; unfortunately her body did not respond in kind. In her twenty-two years, she had never reacted physically to another person. The man held her gaze for an instant and then directed his attention back to his drink. Candy felt a loss once the man looked away. It was a very weird reaction she had to a complete stranger.

She needed to focus on the task at hand. Candy continued further into the restaurant looking for Shirl. She saw her at the rear of the room. A man she had never seen before was seated next to her. He had strawberry-blond curly hair and his body reflected someone who worked out regularly. The man fit with her friend, as no one had before. She'd had one outrageous thought after another since entering this establishment. What was wrong with her? Once again she chided herself. She needed to focus!

Shirl looked up as Candy approached their table. A huge smile crossed her face. Shirl looked absolutely stunning. Her blond hair was pulled back from her face and her light brown eyes sparkled. Candy couldn't remember a time her friend looked happier. Shirl stood and the two friends embraced. Candy felt an overwhelming sense of relief knowing Shirl was all right. She hadn't realized how lost she was not knowing where Shirl and Alex were.

"Where the hell have you been?" Candy asked. Obviously, she wasn't ready to let go of all her anger. She felt Shirl loosening her hold before returning to her seat and grabbing the hand of the man next to her.

"There is so much I need to tell you," Shirl replied. "This is Starc. He is my soul mate." Candy would have laughed if anyone else had uttered those words. Shirl was not a starry-eyed princess who believed in fairy tales. She had said those words with a certainty Candy had never heard in Shirl's voice. For the time being, she would go along with whatever Shirl said. When they were alone, she would cross-examine her friend.

"It is nice to meet you, Candy. Shirl has told me all about you." Starc had a baritone timbre to his tone. He had no discernible accent to place where he was from. But the man was gorgeous, that was for sure.

"We should be going," Shirl said as she stood. She came around the table ready to take Candy to God only knew where. Shirl wore a tunic with leggings and a copper bracelet Candy had never seen. At first glance, it appeared to have multiple etchings on it.

"What in the world are you wearing?" Candy blurted out. A number of responses played in Candy's mind. None of them good. She examined her friend's face and body, trying to identify any camouflaged bruises. Shirl was always self-conscious about her looks, unlike Alex who never worried about physical attributes.

She had been so focused on Shirl, she had momentarily forgotten about her other missing friend. "Where is Alex?"

"Do you trust me, Candy?" Shirl asked. Her friend was dancing around answering her question. It only fueled the suspicions growing in Candy's mind. An uneasiness once again started to consume her.

"Of course, I trust you," Candy said in frustration. By some miracle, she was able to hold back her temper. "But you are beginning to scare me. I want to know where Alex is!"

Shirl paled before her eyes. "I am sure Alex is fine. I need to show you something that will explain everything. Please trust me for the time being."

A pleading look shone in Shirl's eyes. Shirl had never knowingly harmed a soul as far as Candy knew. When they were children, Shirl played the mother hen where she and Alex were concerned. Never in a million years would Shirl do anything to harm either of them. She'd put her faith in her friend.

"This better be good," she said under her breath. Candy did not like playing mental games. As with sports, she liked to see what was coming at her. *Never take your eye off the ball* was her mantra. Reluctantly she followed Shirl and Starc.

Candy was steps away from the exit when she heard "*good luck.*" The words had not been uttered, she was sure of that. They came from within her mind, as if telepathically transmitted. She turned and the man she had seen when she first entered the restaurant was staring at her. He raised his glass, downed the contents, picked up his paper, and started to read. Before she had a chance to question what had just occurred, she was being herded into the back seat of an SUV. Two more strangers were in the front seat. Had she just been kidnapped by some kind of cult?

Candy didn't know if she should call for help or just play along. Shirl reached for her hand and held it for reassurance. That gesture calmed her nerves a bit. No one in the vehicle said a word. There was some nodding and a chuckle, almost as if the occupants were engaged in a conversation. Candy needed to relax and prepare herself for any eventuality. Shirl tightened her grip on her hand.

The men in the front were wearing the same type of outfits Shirl and Starc wore, based on what little she could see. The blond driving had the same type of cuff bracelet Shirl wore. Candy glanced at Starc's wrist. He too had on the same copper jewelry. Everyone wearing identical clothes and bracelets only confirmed Candy's worst fears.

If they were a cult, she decided to wait to make a move until she was with Alex. Alexandra was level headed, although she had once thought the same thing about Shirl. She and Alex would find a way to escape and head straight for the authorities. The fact Alex was not with them told Candy that Alex had not fallen for any of the malarkey Shirl had obviously swallowed.

She felt the SUV slow just before it turned in to one of Boynton Canyon's parking lots leading to the hiking trails. The same spot where Alex had disappeared, according to the police report she had read. Candy barely swallowed past the lump in her throat. Blood rushed through her veins as her pulse rate skyrocketed.

Shirl bounded out of the SUV. She waved for her to follow. Fear momentarily paralyzed Candy. "*Let's go,*" she thought she heard Shirl say, although her lips had not moved.

She was in the middle of a nightmare. That's why she was hearing things not being spoken. Candy would wake up shortly and find herself in her hotel room. This was just another scenario juggling in her mind.

"We mean you no harm, Candy," the man with short black hair and lovely greenish-brown eyes said. He stood just outside the vehicle door Starc had exited. "Some things have to be witnessed to be believed. If I told you who we are and where we are from, you would not believe me. Have you ever seen Shirl look so healthy?" Candy was not sure how to take his reassuring words.

Candy shifted in the back seat and looked at Shirl with a critical eye. Her friend had been suffering debilitating headaches and looked terrible the last time she had seen her. Today Shirl was the poster child for health.

She slid across the seat and exited the SUV. Candy stood next to her friend to get a better look. There were no circles under her eyes or stress lines across her forehead. Her eyes were clear and bright. "How are you feeling, Shirl?" Candy asked suspiciously.

"I have not had a headache since I left," Shirl said. She had not clarified where she had been since she had vanished off the face of the Earth. Once again she decided to take her friend at her word and follow them to wherever they were holding Alex.

The tall slender man with sun-bleached hair who had been driving the car approached. "My name is Darden. It is a pleasure to finally meet you. The man who addressed you earlier is Tarsea. Walk alongside me as we make our way up the trail."

He stepped to the side and extended his arm, indicating for her to join him. Taking one last look around, she realized no other hikers were visible. Candy reluctantly edged closer to Darden. Starc and Shirl led the way, while Tarsea brought up the rear. There was nothing threatening in how they moved or behaved. But Candy pulled on her self-defense training and mentally prepared herself for any aggressive move on their part.

The canyon was absolutely beautiful, but she was too uptight to enjoy her surroundings. Sedona was one of the loveliest places on Earth and it was all lost on her at that moment.

They had walked for twenty minutes when Shirl and Starc stopped. Her friend turned and Candy noticed Shirl's amethyst was glowing. Candy reached out and touched the crystal, bringing a huge smile to Shirl's face. Then Candy noted that Darden and Starc had gems around their necks, also glowing.

"I am a crystal telepath, Candy," Shirl explained. She took Candy's hand and walked with her to a spot on the trail where the air shimmered. "Our late parents came from another universe, parallel to the one that exists in our reality. My mother was the crystal telepath who navigated the portal to bring our parents here. Unfortunately the pollution caused by burning fossil fuels destroyed their telepathic brains before they could escape this world. The headaches I was experiencing would have eventually killed me. I have no headaches in the Troyk universe. Let me take you to your true home, Candy."

At first Candy did not know what to make of the incredible story Shirl had spun. The words rang true, but how that was possible was beyond her comprehension.

Candy stood before the portal, dumbstruck. Shirl's healthy demeanor and the air displacement in front of her were not figments of her imagination. Her friend had read everything she could on string theory and alternate universes, but Candy never believed that crap. Now, the evidence was right in front of her and she had problems wrapping her brain around the fact it was all true. Or maybe she was right all along and she was dreaming. This could not be reality.

"What about Alex?" Candy inquired. Even with the overwhelming evidence before her eyes about the existence of multiple dimensions, Candy could not let go of her concern for their absent friend. Could Alex have been pulled into one of these event horizons and ended up God knows where? Had she literally vanished off the face of the Earth?

"I am sure Alex is fine where she is," Shirl answered. Candy did not like the vagueness of her friend's reply. "Your headaches will start soon, if they have not already. You are two years younger than I am and my headaches started about the age you are now. This world is a death sentence for us if we stay. Our life expectancy here is twenty-five years, if we are lucky." Shirl took Candy's hand and squeezed it. The little girl she once was knew she needed to follow Shirl wherever she led. "We can walk through the portal together."

Candy was still absorbing the existence of the portal and parallel universes. It was true, she was starting to get headaches. If in fact she was dreaming, what harm would it do to go through the portal? She tightened her grasp on her friend's hand indicating her consent.

The men entered the portal first. Candy took a deep breath, closed her eyes, and stepped in alongside her friend.

About the Author

When Evelyn Lederman retired from her career as an insurance executive, she cheerfully anticipated the freedom to finally spend as much time reading as she'd always wanted. The twist in her story came when as-yet unwritten characters started cropping up in her thoughts, asking her to tell their stories. Now, she spends her days in Florida on the beach... with her laptop.

'The Chameleon Soul Mate', 'The Crystal Telepath', and 'The Warrior Woman' are the first three books in her paranormal sci-fi romance series, Worlds Apart. 'Nightshade' is the first book in her new series, The Nightshade Saga.

Keep up to date with her at EvelynLederman.com or on Facebook. Contact her at evelynlauthor@gmail.com